Quantum (

In the
Eleventh Dimension

Within the Eleventh Dimension
Both Time & Chronology Cease To Be
And A Myriad Of Impossibilities Become Possible...

13 short stories

SCIENCE FICTION ANTHOLOGIES

QUANTUM CHRONICLES
IN THE
ELEVENTH DIMENSION

Anthony Fucilla

Published 2013 by arima publishing

www.arimapublishing.com

ISBN 978 1 84549 583 1

Printed and bound in the United Kingdom

Typeset in Garamond

Swirl is an imprint of arima publishing.

arima publishing
ASK House, Northgate Avenue
Bury St Edmunds, Suffolk IP32 6BB
t: (+44) 01284 700321

www.arimapublishing.com

Cover Design: PJP

Anthony was born in London on the 6th of January 1975, from Italian parents. He was training to become a professional footballer in Spain with Atletico Marbella, and also had various trials around Europe. He studied Theology and Philosophy, and also entered the field of Engineering, becoming an ROV Pilot. Anthony is now a Science Fiction writer. His books consist of short stories containing elements of Philosophy and Theology.

CONTENTS

13 Sci-fi Tales

In the world of Sci-fi, reality becomes a fantasy and fantasy a reality. It allows us to dream for a time; our imagination wanders into a realm of impossibility; it breaks the barriers of logic, the summit of our knowledge, and enters a new dimension......

Metallic Cosmos
Clegg Willis, human, one of few alive, dwells within a world where only A-class Robots rule.

Electro Domestics of the Future
After a twelve-year sentence is cut short, Craig De Lucas returns to Earth from Mars. The government has handed him a stern task.

Molecular Alteration
Jack Webster is a simple-minded old man who dreams of rejuvenation; the closest thing to immortality, man's greatest quest since time began.

Mechanical Eyes
Engineer Michael Richards battles against a dream; a dream which he is convinced is real. Is it all the manufacture of his mind, a chemically-induced occurrence, or are there other hidden truths? Which is the greater reality: the world we know or the one in our dreams?

Chronology
Two men are catapulted ahead in time...Somewhere between the sky and the Earth lies a doorway into another world.

The Storm Chaser
Al Dennis, storm chaser, finds himself torn from the world he knew. His whole identity is now called into question.

No Mars Redemption
Gary Pope, resident of the Red Planet, longs to see the new Mars.

Time Report
Reinhardt Brewster files in the Time Report...65 years of age and deemed fit to live out the rest of his life.

Invader
Chris Nicholson journeys to a planet and soon discovers he's not alone.

Visions of the Future
On a space flight, Lawrence Colt suddenly awakens.

Ganymede Project
A genetically engineered man is sent to Ganymede on a terraforming project.

Ripple Effect
Can a simple journey back in Time alter the present?

The Winds of Mars
An ex-intergalactic soldier reflects on the meaning of life.

Introduction

This book is comprised of thirteen short stories. Of all the thirteen tales, Molecular Alteration is one of the most challenging, as it relates to man's deepest struggle from within: the ageing process. The story is purely Science Fiction, but contains elements of philosophy and theology. Why am I here? Where is my life journey taking me? As a Christian, I feel it is essential to ask such questions of ourselves.

The journey of life takes us through various events; some we hold dear, others we choose to forget. Is it plausible to believe that all of it is just a weird, senseless journey into nothingness? Or at the end, is there a reason why? What is it that holds the universe of matter together and sets life into motion? If a man truly searches for such answers, he will find. Once our lives and hearts are open and receptive to the things of God, all that we see around us makes sense and fits perfectly into place; the puzzle of life becomes unravelled, pure and translucent. Our journey turns from senseless to meaningful and one which is filled with both happiness and peace; a peace which transcends human understanding.

When gazing out into the night sky at the heavenly spheres, or sitting staring at the ocean towards the distant horizon, surely then you begin to comprehend just how Awesome and Beautiful the LORD is. HIS Majesty and Power are surely displayed in the wonders of the universe and in the planet which thrives with life; the planet which we call home.

Metallic Cosmos

HE AWOKE to the roar of a passing interplanetary ship exceeding its legal velocity, its blinding lights flickering in the cold night sky, filtering into the bedroom of where Clegg Willis lay. Through the balcony window lay the city of San Francisco, bustling with sounds which boomed from day till night.

Slipping out from his hydro-bed, he snapped on the power of his arc-shaped side lamp. Instantly, the room was filled with light; an amber light, soft and calming. In a little while Clegg would be back at work. It wasn't easy for the remaining humans to dwell within a world where A-Class Robots ruled. After the war, man was subjected to the authority of machines; at least, the ones which remained.

Rising to his feet, he stretched in his loose-fitting white pyjamas. In the corner of the room, the vision set sprang into life, triggered by his faint moving motion. A cold, clipped formality. Across the screen an A-Class Robot sat dialoguing with another of its own kind.

"Conscience is an interesting phenomenon; it lies partly in the psychological realm."

Clegg smirked in ironic amusement. *What the hell do they know about conscience?* he thought to himself. *After all, they are nothing more than machines, programmed to think and act accordingly, a creation of man's innate knowledge and highly developed faculties.*

Inching over to his bedroom table, he picked up his glass-bottled vita-drink; a strong concoction of liquids and finely ground herbs. The same sharp buzz swept through him as always as he poured it down greedily. Sleep began to dissolve as the potent mixture awoke him, burning his throat and stinging his eyes, yet allowing him to condense his nocturnal dreams and scattered thoughts into a semblance of rationality.

Making his way to the closet, he slipped out of his pyjamas, leaving them lying on the tiled floor in a crinkled heap. Hastily, he began changing into his grey uniform, printed across with the word, 'HUMAN'. From the corner of his eye, he caught a brief yet decisive glimpse of the time; it wouldn't be long before his nightshift commenced, labouring away at the construction site with the other resentful humans. Briskly, he gathered up his set of three-dimensional chess putting it into his pocket, along with his greatest prize of all, his tiny disc.

Before long, he had descended from the apartment, out into the night street. Sharp, colourful city light flooded over him, glowing from beyond, cutting off the futile flickers of starlight; the waves of city sound had now somewhat nullified.

In the distance, he could see an R-Cab approaching; hurriedly, he waved it down. As the robot driver acknowledged his signalling, it pulled over to the curb, halting smoothly. The door slid open; Clegg squeezed in. The robot turned, its eyes dilating; its metal-shaped mouth opened with metallic dignity.

"WHERE CAN I TAKE YOU, HUMAN?"

"Wilburn Street," he rasped in reply, with a detectable hint of resentment in his voice; at least, clearly detectable to the wide-eyed, perceptive robot. Its receptors triggered off an electric impulse that changed its unusually friendly mood into unconcealed hostility. An expression of sullen distaste spread over its features. With the grippers of a fingeroid shape, it then held the lever forward, driving away to the set destination.

At the construction site, the R-Cab stopped. There was a smell of dust commingling with the faint pungent scent of humans. In a world of odourless machines, the human aroma stood out boldly. In swift motion, the robot swivelled its chest around, leaving the lower part of its frame facing forward.

"That'll be forty credits." Its metal face then froze, glowing with an almost organic eloquence, as if it had transmuted from an inanimate machine into a living being. Exploring about in his pockets, Clegg pulled out his card, placing it into the credit register. Within seconds it flashed. Next, the door slid open; he stepped out. Before him stood a fellow human, a Filipino worker, filled with dust and dirt, almost lost in the gloom of night but for the bright lights shining down onto the construction site.

"Clegg…"

"Yes," he replied with unassuming knowledge, his thin brows raised in expectancy.

"You're wanted at the office…apparently it's your monthly review…"

A hot breath of air came out in a haze from his mouth, fading into the cold night. His English contained no remnant of an accent.

"They certainly know how to pick the time! These machines have no sense of chronology…but of course, what can we expect? Thanks, Bob."

Bob turned and walked away, leaving in his wake the stench of perspiration, the smell of backbreaking labour.

A swirl of dust gushed into the air as the turbo drills activated, sending shock waves along the surface of the earth with deafening shrills. Further on down the street stood a skyscraper. A pyramid-shaped structure, it had the mark of human engineering; a monumental tower stained with sweat and blood of human hands. It was distinct, almost shimmering with a silvery brilliance. Steadily Clegg began walking over, the moon shining brighter across his face as it escaped the night mists. It really bothered him having to spend that same long tedious hour sitting before his robotic employers as they muttered cold unemotional sounds, which of course were nothing more to him than electrical signals converted into acoustic energy; metallic junk.

On the twentieth floor, the elevator halted, and with a faint whoosh, the hydraulic-powered door slid open. He stepped out into a familiar reception area. A robot guard roamed; a pale tower of metal and plastic. Briskly, it was alerted to the presence of a human, as its highly developed sensors, operating at maximum velocity, detected an energy field....Clegg's. With a sharp turn, the robot scanned down his image with its photocell eyes, Clegg remaining hushed as always.

"Human, don't you realise you're out of your jurisdiction? Who gave you authorisation?" Its fine metallic tone held cold reserve, tinged with immeasurable hostility.

"I was told I had my monthly review..." His chin sank, resting against his chest. He then looked up, coloured in reddish but controlled anger. In the years since Humans had become second class citizens, he had learned to repress the impulse to confront an A-Class Robot; it was a federal offence, one which had devastating consequences - sometimes termination of life.

The robot raised its twisted steel arm, and spoke into a transmitter which was fixed across its wrist. *"We have a Human here for its monthly review."* A voice bleeped back icily, *"Send it through."*

Walking down a winding hallway, Clegg could see his little miserable human reflection scattered across the silvery entrance door. He took a breath; a long, steady breath. Regaining an element of composure, he held his hand before the code beam; the door faded, he stepped in, and the door quickly reformed behind him. Immediately, a voice uttered from beyond the dazzling lights, *"Mr Willis, take a seat."* Shifting his eyes with disgust, Clegg sat resting his elbows against a white desk, clasping his hands, the robot sitting on the opposite side, sparkling brilliantly under the powerful overhead lights. Its eyes dilated, zooming in.

"And how are we today, Mr Willis?" the robot sputtered out sharply, almost with a hint of sarcasm.

There was no response, then a moment of hesitation. *"SPEAK UP, HUMAN,"* the robot demanded. After a solemn pause, Clegg replied with reluctance. *"I'm good, Sir, real good."* Those same familiar words gripped his insides with utter revulsion. *"An artefact,"* he thought to himself, *"you're nothing but an artefact created as a result of advanced human minds, the greatest prize - ironic as it seems - of human understanding, the summit of our knowledge."* The paradox was that it had backfired with mind-blowing destruction; these machines now ruled with an amazing intellectual awareness. They had mastered the art of dialectics and defeated the creators, standing tall in a world where only they ruled.

Before any further dialogue was exchanged, the robot reached under the desk. There was a clank, the sound of metal, as if the robot were manufacturing something. Clegg became apprehensive and curious; this wasn't part of the mundane systematic routine. His curiosity rose. *"What's going on?"* he said sharply, his voice almost fading into extinction. There was no reply. Clegg remained hushed, perceiving the hint; after all, he didn't want to overstep his mark. The robot then rose, holding a device; complex-looking, with a trailing wire. The device was alien to Clegg. He repressed the impulse to enquire, as his curiosity briskly transformed into outright fear; yet he muttered not. His eyes grew large and questioning. The robot instantly computed that Clegg was concerned, yet it held cold reserve towards him. After all, what could an inanimate machine understand about pity; a value of which robots, no matter how sophisticated, were devoid.

Clegg sat back in his seat, contemplating, staring grimly at the wall as if in search of refuge. *"Mr Willis, can I have your complete attention?"* In swift motion, he deflected his focus from the wall to the robot. With straining effort, he tried to appear calm in order to retain his dignity, but his face failed to respond. His eyes widened with acceptance, conveying all he was feeling, as if they spoke of the chemical reactions that were taking place within him with muted urgency.

Placing the device before Clegg, the robot then plugged the wire into an electrical outlet. Instantly there was a dim smell of negative ions as they surged from the power supply. The device came alive, two hazy blue pencil beams of light shooting towards Clegg's face, feeding directly into his eyes, yet with no detrimental biological effect on him. A disc scanner hummed away, recording. From across the desk, the robot activated a switch, which in turn dimmed the room into virtual darkness.

"*Right, Mr. Willis, keep your eyes focused on the blue lights as steady as you can; try to avoid flinching.*"

"*I'm not mechanical, Sir, I'm physical,*" he replied, somewhat sarcastically. It seemed as if the barriers of respect were slowly subsiding between man and machine, as Clegg began to release that ever-increasing negative energy.

"*What is this, an eye test? Are you measuring dilation? This is certainly a most unconventional way of completing a review.*"

"*Keep quiet, Human. Now, I have a series of questions which you need to answer as briskly as you can; reaction time is an important factor.*"

Sweat broke out across Clegg's face; a drop burnt his left eye, but he fought it, and did not give in to the urge to flinch. He could sense the robot staring at him from beyond the darkness, analysing him as if he were an animal.

"*Mr. Willis, this is your first question.*" There was a moment of silence. "*Tell me, do you enjoy working as a construction labourer?*"

The robot began studying the small screen on the back of the device. It was scanning Clegg's brain, gathering information and registering it. A wave pattern then appeared on the screen. A high frequency wave. The robot deduced the human was aggravated. Frigid perspiration rose to the surface of Clegg's skin. He swallowed; the heat and tension combined, leaving a poisonous bitter taste in his mouth. He knew damn right how to answer that question, but of course he refrained.

"*Yes, yes I do, Sir.*" He bit his tongue.

The robot studied the screen again; the wave pattern was coming in distorted, fluctuating violently with high amplitude, a sign of soaring stress levels. The minor delay in his response and the pitch in his voice indicated to the robot that it was a false response. Clegg's mind was obviously concentrating on other factors; so much for the distinction between an authentic living human and a robot.

"*Second question. Tell me, what do you think of your superiors?*"

A matter of seconds passed. Clegg's mind was reeling, his heart pounding fiercely in and out of rhythm, neural adrenaline surging through him, triggering an outbreak of fury. Then, pulling away from the light source, he stood up and blasted out after years of suppression.

"*Damn it! I've had enough of this! I won't live a second longer like a chained animal, regardless of the consequences. I despise you and all that you stand for… You're nothing but a piece of machinery; a human tool; an artificial construct; an inanimate object mimicking an animate one… you're nothing more than a creation of my ancestors…unlike what the twisted indoctrinated myths state, those very ones manufactured by the pre-war A-Class robots. All that you feel and know is artificial, a simulated world of which you don't exist……"*

The room lights suddenly activated. He paused, his face red, his chest rising and falling as he puffed away, eyes wide, hands shaking.

"Good, Mr Willis! Finally, after many years, the first human since the war reveals his true emotions with unconcealed clarity. Your face, Mr Willis, your face is filled with hatred, an emotion which we are devoid of… yet one you have the good sense to control. After years of study and observation we are still far from understanding the mechanics of the human mind; how a complex bundle of atoms, molecules, amino acids makes a human being, the cardinal mystery of life. To allow for human expression would be more beneficial for us, if we are ever going to fully understand the bio-chemistry of the human anatomy; the differences between flesh and machine."

Clegg remained startled, surprised to see the robot's philosophical response to his fierce verbal attack. He had committed a federal offence, yet it had seemed to go unpunished - at least, the robot's reaction led him to believe as much. He exhaled in absolute, almost convulsive, relief. His adrenal gland, by degrees, ceased pumping its several secretions into his bloodstream; his heartbeat returned to normal, his breathing with it.

"Confused? Aren't you, Mr. Willis? Indeed, you should be; your reaction is punishable by death. I'm sure you know the laws which govern the state?"

With his eyes Clegg signalled his understanding. The perceptive robot registered and computed.

"Speak, Mr Willis; you're free to speak without the fear of a penalty."

Again, a wave of surprise swept over Clegg, nullifying his remaining fears. He regained composure and sat.

"What more is there to convey? Living under the rule of machines is not an easy thing to accept… maker subjected to the authority of the created. I've had to watch in grim agony, while your kind wiped out human existence but for a few; along with it, our culture and traditions, something which you can't relate to and never will. I saw it all dissolve away into radioactive particles, all before my very eyes.

All that you are is a result of human craft and engineering; your reality, your universe, that which you control is coming to you from a minuscule unit inside your head. If it were shut down your world would cease to be."

Clegg opened his mouth ready to fire more heated metal-stripping words at the somewhat subdued robot, who by now seemed amazingly withdrawn in the presence of a human. The robot stood rocking back on its heels, head down.

"There can be only one ruler, Mr. Willis, just like there is one life-bearing sun."

"Yes, indeed," he said bravely. *"But how can you pretend to ignore the one absolute fact?"* He paused. *"Without human intervention there would be no you, or indeed any of your kind."*

The robot extended its left gripper, scratching its slender metal head reflectively. Its photocell eyes shut, masked by a pale lens, then flipped open seconds later.

"Despite what you say, humans never showed the right leadership skills to maintain a complex world; we, on the other hand, are able to keep the cosmos functioning systematically, smoothly, everything in order. We robots know our place, and execute all our duties with perfection and precision."

"Indeed you do; everything is completely linear with your kind. No room for expression or thought, no room for flamboyant thinkers. This is the main difference between flesh and machine, between an artistic mind and one which is purely intellectual. Us humans can sing, cook and eat, something your kind will never know. We have highly developed emotions, a refined aesthetic awareness; we are sensitive to sound, colour and texture, and are able to make radical distinctions between beauty and ugliness, good and bad. We are not manufactured, but created biologically. We can multiply in abundance without the need to fret. Mankind is nothing short of a living miracle; to understand the mechanics of the human anatomy is to unravel the mystery of life. Surely there is no room for denial in that mechanical mind of yours. We humans are so very special."

There was an interval of complete silence, a minute of brief contemplation. The robot sat gazing across the room at Clegg, its face fixed and stern with a human-like acknowledgement, its eyes shifting with curiosity, solemn and half astonished.

"There is now no going back, Mr. Willis. The past is clearly over, and nothing can be altered. Tell me, what is it that you would like to see in the future?"

"For the few humans that remain, I would like to see us catapulted into our rightful seat, into our rightful position, where we are not treated like slaves and at the very least live in equality with you robots. But that, of course, is just wishful thinking; a hypothetical scenario that will never be."

There was a strange glow in Clegg's eyes, a yearning, distant look. Pictures began to form, lighting his mind. He could see images of the early days when humans ran the cosmos; robots didn't even exist, or the few that did were tightly under human control and supervision. It felt like it was just the other day that he had sat in the underground labs watching fellow men constructing robots out of a baffling maze of circuitry and gadgets. For a second he smiled, but it faded promptly. He captured further images; the war, robots snaking through the ruins and ash, emerging as masters, building up their post-war society, swarming over planet Earth and entering into the cosmos, constructing complex cities; humans working away feverishly as slaves covered in filth and dust, the stench of despair and defeat in the air. All human power, knowledge and culture lost in one big explosion, dissolving away into nothingness, into the void with no chance of any return or reconciliation.

The robot's photocell eyes grew wide, as if registering Clegg's thoughts with a seemingly telepathic faculty. It then spoke out abruptly, yet with unusual diplomacy.

"Mr Willis, before I dismiss you, is there any other point you would like to make?"

"Yes," he replied with a smile, the smile continuing to glow across his face, as if he were about to reveal the cardinal mystery of life.

"This is our world; Earth belongs to us. It always has and always will, no matter what."

An uneasy chill shot through the robot, electrically induced. It hesitated.

"Here," Clegg said, pulling out the tiny history-disc from his pocket. *"I've kept this hidden away for years, waiting for the right moment, and now it has finally come. It was handed down to me by my father. Take it, analyse it systemically, the way you know best. Feed it into your scanner, then you'll understand what I mean. I can tell from your module number that you were manufactured after the war. I am correct, am I not?"*

The robot remained in stunned silence and signalled 'yes' by nodding its head somewhat reluctantly.

"Once you watch the disc you'll never be the same, never. It will show you what it means to be human, something that your kind will never comprehend. It will show you the world as it once was under our rule and dictatorship, in all its splendour and beauty; the one which was so tragically taken from us......"

"The review has ended. Mr. Willis, please make your way out," the robot said with a subdued acceptance. Clegg hesitated. Placing the disc shakily on the desk, he then stood and made his way to the door.

"Oh, Mr. Willis..." Clegg paused, turning his head in apprehension. *"You can go home now, I'm sure the review has taken more out of you than expected. Indeed, Mr. Willis, we robots will never know what it truly means to be human; fatigue is something which we can't relate to."*

Incredibly, a smile manifested itself across the robot's face, as it extended its left gripper, pointing it towards the door, warmly. It amazed Clegg to see such warm interaction with a robot, especially in the prevailing circumstances. Silently he turned and made his way out in utter astonishment, the transition showing on his face.

He awoke and it was daylight. Sleep promptly dissolved as a dazzle of sunlight flinched his eyes open. Pensively, he lay there in his hydro-bed with a sense of partially restored pride and optimism, sheet covers creased over his body. Maybe there was a way back; a way to gather the remaining humans and make a stand - at least to obtain equal rights. His mind was gripped with the antics of the night passed. He still couldn't believe what had transpired; it was like a blurred dream roaming in the back of his mind.

As he slipped out of the hydro-bed, the vision set activated, glowing into life. Slowly and wearily, he made his way to the balcony, parting the sliding doors before him. Instantly, he was met with the cold morning air lapping over him. It felt good to be alive and human, he thought to himself; an odd sensation of which he had been devoid since childhood. Like an arc of pure fire, an interplan ship shot across the morning sky, breaking his dawn drowsiness. The burning orb of the sun reflected yellow light across the city, the same life-filling light which had beamed down for centuries past. The steel micro-chip jungle gleamed and sparkled; everything in mathematical order, robots in motion throughout. From his bird's-eye view he could see their tiny dwindling metal heads bobbing up and down as they made their way to work methodically, surface vehicles cramming the streets, noisy sounds and the complex tangle and confusion of city life. Then, from below, he caught the desperate cries of a human child.

"Daddy, that horrible robot just called me human...why can't they stop rubbing it in?"

"Don't worry, son...it will be okay, just be proud of what you are. You'll snap back...You'll see."

Clegg's face faded from sympathetic concern to outright disgust. No wonder robots roamed the streets with such arrogance. What hope was there for the remaining humans dwelling in a world where only A-class robots ruled?

Electro Domestics of the Future

Craig De Lucas sat in his oxygen-controlled cell gazing towards the mountains of Mars; a cold reddish desert, bleak and hostile; Olympus Mons towering high, stretching into the atmosphere of the Martian world. In the distance there was a loud shattering roar like distant thunder. *'Must be a transport ship returning from a nearby planet,'* he muttered to himself. His face was moved with emotion as he reflected back to his days on Earth, now a distant memory. He shut his eyes and images from the past brilliantly lit his mind. He could almost feel the enveloping presence of the other world which was once home… Earth.

The sudden sound of beating footsteps broke his concentration. Instantly he was back to reality, the landscape and the mundane surroundings of the prison cell conspiring to remind him where he was. With a faint hum the cell door opened, sliding into the ground. Stepping through the opening was a man. Finely dressed, professional looking; his attire alone suggested he was from Earth, his eyes and his motion so distinct. Behind him, a prison guard held a blast gun with unconcealed hostility. *"Hey, De Lucas, get up! You've got a visitor."*

Instinctively, Craig directed his attention towards the well-suited man, rubbing his hand across his bristled chin, his eyes glazed with reluctant admiration.

"Do you need me here, Mr Ryan?" the grey-uniformed guard mumbled.

"No, that won't be necessary."

The guard walked away, the cell door closing behind him and bolting into place.

"I guess you're here to read me my rights," Craig muttered sarcastically, sitting on his bed.

"No, not exactly." Ryan moved towards a chair facing a lacquered desk. *"Craig, please…take a seat."*

Standing, Craig walked over; there was a rancid stench of sweat. He sat folding his arms with disinterest; his legs sprawled above the desk. A deep shadow was cast under his hollowed-out cheeks, as the dim cell light shone across his face.

"You're probably wondering who I am, and why I'm here.…"

There was a long pause, as they both exchanged piercing eye contact.

"Craig, how would you like to have your name cleared…your freedom…a chance to return to Earth; live an ordinary life again? I believe you've served three years of a twelve-year sentence, labouring, withering away slowly……Interested?"

Craig sat up, his face alight, dull eyes igniting with sudden hunger. Gently, he rested his elbows against the desk, clasping his hands expectantly.

"What is this, a joke?"

"No, Craig, this is no joke," Ryan replied, sitting with an elaborated casualness.

"I've spent years locked up in this cell, millions and millions of kilometres away from Earth…I committed no crime…Has it taken the authorities this long to realise…?" His tone rose, rippling with profound irritation, his face set with grim determination.

"Your eccentric scientific research could have potentially caused millions of deaths on Earth had it not been for government intervention. Your love of science almost led to a catastrophic disaster…you did not adhere to government safety regulations. The penalty was severe, even if your work was motivated with the best of intentions…"

There was a moment of silence and hesitation.

"My name's Bill Ryan. I'm here on behalf of the GSS, the Government Secret Service, to be exact…"

Nervous sweat dripped down Craig's face. He regained poise.

He raised a finger to his lips as a measure of curiosity came over him.

"Back on Earth, a team of scientists have been constructing a number of highly sophisticated robots; Android is the official term, to be precise, capable of indulging in the most complex of tasks with a seemingly telepathic faculty far superior to man. Like any human, they are biological, made from complex cells; a bundle of amino acids, blood filling veins, and natural skin covering natural flesh. Yet, deeply embedded within these Androids is a vast array of wires, miniaturised components, intricate circuit boards and powerful motors. Earth now houses hundreds of thousands of these biomechanical machines. But we now have a serious problem…

"Unfortunately, many Androids have started a revolt against humans, a bloody mutiny. They want total power and control. An underground group is growing in number. The Androids are no different from the Bolsheviks, or the Roundheads. Throughout history there has always been a group that wanted to lead mankind. Besides, the Androids believe they are superior to humans in every respect; hence, it is natural, in their opinion, that they should lead us, since they view humans as an inferior species."

"Are they superior?" Craig asked, eagerly leaning forward, his body tense.

"Let's not de-gravitate from the point. Yes, Androids do excel in most fields; humans in others. But there's no way we can allow them to take control. They must be stopped and wiped out. There is a way, perhaps the only way, to exterminate them…The easiest solution would be to create a virus - human-friendly, of course - that when

released into the atmosphere would kill them off. We considered other methods, none realistic. According to Professor Maitao, head of New Tec, creator of the Androids, a virus is the only solution."

"Why me?"

"Craig, despite what happened, I find that a strange question. Given your experience and background, as an eminent genius in the field of virology, we felt it was something that you could help us with. You have quite a mouth-opening CV. You are the only one who could make this possible...accomplish the task. We tried others, scientists from all over the US. The National Research Institute set a chain of experiments into motion...they all failed."

Craig was gripped with a sense of controlled euphoria and deep emotion. The trace of a smile twitched across his lips. Bill Ryan continued.

"There's even talk the Androids are now capable of replicating themselves, illegally, of course. Apparently, some have the technological know-how and means. Where and how, I don't know; perhaps in some underground laboratory..."

He swallowed, wiping his forehead.

"The number of government-registered Androids now probably is inaccurate. Humans are losing control of the situation rapidly. If our intentions were revealed, we could have a grim time of it. Whatever we do, it must remain top secret, strictly confidential. No one outside of top government officials must know. If word leaks out, it will be disastrous; half the city of LA is now filled with them!"

"How and why, exactly, were they made?"

"In factories guided by the company New Tec Robotics. They were made to assist humans, mostly on outer space projects. However, the law does permit them a certain amount of freedom and equality, and independence to work in almost any capacity they see fit. Naturally, certain ones were made for a particular function, but as a whole they have rights just like us. They are, however, unable to work within the police force and government, it's illegal...only humans can function in those capacities. So what do you say?" Bill Ryan lifted both hands with suggestion.

"Deal is we fly you back to Earth on a private government ship...provide you with all the essential information and data, then it's up to you. The chip implanted in your head will enable us to monitor your movements – obviously, you understand why."

"So what's the catch?" Craig asked bluntly.

"No catch... But you can't fail us. Failure means a prompt return to Mars to see out the remainder of your sentence; success means the chance to remain on Earth. Just give me the word and you'll be out of here by tomorrow night. All your provisions will be taken care of... clothes, transport, apartment, money..."

With a cold, hard expression he held his face towards the ground and then looked up. His eyes widened, his face glowing with animation.

"When do I leave...?"

At the Mars Interplanetary Spaceport, Craig was escorted through customs by a number of police troopers in their distinctive red uniforms. At the end of a long ship connecting tunnel he arrived at the entrance to the departure gate. After being briefly searched by officials, he passed under a security device; a highly advanced x-ray machine. In the corner, Bill Ryan stood waiting, holding a briefcase, dressed in an elegant grey suit, smoking with a suave confidence. Across the wall was a wide shifting colour screen......DESTINATION EARTH. Bill strolled over.

"I see you're all set to go...It won't be long now before we're away..."

Craig was soundless, his mind engaging in deep thought. A uniformed guard walked over holding a security-beam device, waving it at them.

"Travel cards please..."

From his jacket pocket, Bill flung out the clearance cards, slipping them into the guard's hands. After a few frustrating minutes, the guard passed them back with a big slanting smile; it appeared manufactured.

"Have a pleasant journey, Sir."

Through the thick glass window, Craig saw a number of ships preparing for descent, hovering above the surface of the planet; others were dimly visible in the distance, gliding between mountain ranges. His heart began to beat heavily as the burning reality of his predicament became all the more real.

Walking up to the entrance of the ship, there were sounds of the inspection crew making final checks before take-off. Controlled atmosphere began to hiss in; the sound grew louder until it was clearly audible. With a faint whoosh the door retracted back, and a youngish looking space host walked out. He was a short, slender man with delicate features, from an obvious oriental background; his hair fine, black and evenly parted.

"Hi, Mr Ryan....Take-off will be as scheduled."

As they entered, they sat on the white coloured pressure seats; take-off shock absorbers, latching safety belts around them. With the closing of hydraulic doors, all sounds from outside the ship were cut off with immediate effect. Abruptly the ship came to life. Visible down the aisle was the control-room. Two space navigators sat dressed in their familiar grey uniforms, manipulating switches, mumbling away. The control-room was a complex mixture of dials, buttons and flickering lights.

For a brief moment an alarm sounded. Atmospheric pressure had declined. Seconds later, it stabilised. Then silence. As the lights inside the ship began to fade, a huge screen lit up before them; a navigator's face formed, giving a brief account of the journey. Then a satellite image of Earth followed; a green distant sphere rotating slowly, engulfed in cloud. Craig looked on eagerly, repressing his emotions. He pictured the ocean, the endless miles of foaming water…great mountains, a planet saturated in life of countless forms; complex and intricate, memories of green.

The mere thought of returning excited him. He brilliantly recalled his time spent researching in the dense jungles of South America, the Amazon steaming with fetid rot, coiled, gleaming reptiles moving through the marshes, the endless varieties of life; it briefly deflected him from the task at hand. Next the image across the screen began to magnify, plunging deeper into planet Earth towards the US. A city then came into sharp view. He could see skyscrapers, broad streets, people going about their daily activities. In a little while he would be among them. Destination Los Angeles…

The blast jets ignited with a loud shattering roar, the ground rumbling under them. With an awesome burst of energy the ship took off, disappearing into the thin Martian atmosphere. The red globe that was Mars grew steadily smaller. Beneath lay endless miles of oxidised rock and gaping craters as far as the eye could see. They were now out of sight, voyaging into free space, free of gravity, the fundamental force which held the universe of matter within its grip. On and on they went, lost in the vastness of space, journeying between distant spheres, alien worlds; a boundless universe which stretched off into infinity.

At the LA Interplan Spaceport the ship arrived after a five-day journey. It was now 20:25 Earth time. The cold orb of the moon appeared and vanished as dense red clouds of sulphuric acid passed above the sky line. Walking into the entrance lounge, there were endless crowds of people, a torrent of noise and activity. Craig gazed around in excitement, like a lost fugitive getting back to grips with the complex tangle and chaotic confusion of the world. Suddenly an amplified female voice blared, 'Welcome to LA.' The sound came in from all directions with finesse and clarity, yet somewhat muffled in his fatigued mind.

"What time is it?" he asked, running his fingers through his sandy blond hair, his eyes staring like two dark coals. Bill consulted his watch, dials glowing yellow.

"20.45. Don't worry…it won't take you long to acclimatise back to Earth time."

Passing through customs, they entered the arrivals lounge. At the end of a long hall was a man waving over; a distinctive eye-capturing slash across his forehead ending at his cheek. His rain jacket was wet from the ongoing downpour.

"That's my work colleague Fred Burton," Bill said, increasing his pace.

"Hi Fred, this is Professor Craig De Lucas."

They shook hands firmly. Fred smirked, staring at him eye to eye, as he lowered his rain hat in greeting.

"I hope you had a pleasant trip," he said flatly with his husky, smoke-drenched voice.

"Yes, I did."

"Come…Let's make our way."

Walking out into the rain, a light grey hover-car was parked up to the side. From a control device Fred flipped the doors open; instantly it lit up. Craig studied him acutely for a brief moment; there was something oddly different about him; his motion and facial expressions, his eyes hard, polished with an inorganic quality. Across the street in green flashing lights, an advertisement board stood: MARS VACATIONS.

Entering the hover-car it rose from the surface, gaining altitude rapidly, the ground and familiar city roads slowly disappearing into tiny dwindling specks. On and on they ascended into vast clouds of the night, guide-lights penetrating into the dense atmosphere. The city of LA now appeared as an endless cluster of luminous flickering dots. From the distance there was a sound, a great booming roar. An oncoming police-air-vehicle, immense in diameter, glided overhead monitoring air traffic, lights flashing blue and red.

Craig lay back, dazed from the rapid ascent. He couldn't quite believe how his life had altered; it all seemed surreal to him returning to Earth in such bizarre circumstances… *I am really here*, he thought to himself. He began glancing up into the night sky as if for confirmation. From the front seat Bill turned, gazing at him. In his hand he held a small bag with a dangling long strap.

"Here, take this," he said, his eloquent tone now jaded with noticeable fatigue. *"The contents inside include your entry card to the apartment, a wristwatch*

and some relevant documentation. *You will also find a powerful handgun just for your protection.*"

Craig pulled out the watch, examining it with meticulous precision. It was weightless, silver coloured, both analogue and digital. Placing it on, its adjustable straps moulded perfectly around his slender wrist. Bill rumbled on...

"*In terms of transportation we have supplied you with a hover-bike. I'm sure you know how to get around on one of those; it has an inbuilt voice navigation system. Finally, you've to report to me by 1pm tomorrow at my office. We will discuss where and when you will commence your research. We will have to correspond as much as possible.*"

Within a short period of time they began a swift descent, wide city roads coming into sharp focus, sounds growing louder, a sea of unknown faces displayed all around. The surroundings were somewhat familiar to him. He searched his mind, recalling the location brightly.

Landing beside a towering line of skyscrapers, the back door flipped open. Across the street was an oriental food bar, TIGERS flashing blue. He stepped out, grabbing his bag. A burst of frigid wind struck him, half turning him around.

Above him, the moon grew brighter as it escaped the mists and entered a patch of clear sky. The window lowered, Bill leaned out into the mild yet unending rain.

"*It's good to be back, hey?*"

He smiled, his tired eyes whipping into sudden life.

"*See you tomorrow...Make sure you get plenty of rest.*"

Craig stood there for a time, absorbing the city air. He then had the sudden urge to walk around, despite his fatigue. Down a long street he noticed there was an open air mart, one of the many city trans-planet marts, where merchandise from the rich colonies of Mars, Ganymede and Titan was sold. People stood around, sampling and pricing, chatting and discussing.

The next morning he was in the headquarters of a government building. Bill Ryan sat facing him on the opposite side of a desk. Heaped across the desk were a litter of cigarette butts, various documents and folders.

"*So Craig, I hope it's all clear to you now. Don't forget you're meeting Professor Maitao this evening. He's quite a man, the Director of New Tec...designer and maker of the Androids. He will undoubtedly fill you in with some important information, imperative towards your research.*"

Bill rolled up his sleeve, consulting his wristwatch. He then pulled out a long cigar and lit up with his initialled lighter. The flame blew out; he lit again, shielding it with his hand, the coal of his cigar glowing red hot. Smoke filled the office, blending in with the pale light.

"Well, I think I've covered all that I needed to. You're free to leave," he said huskily with his smoke-filled mouth.

"Okay, we'll be in touch. Thanks Mr Ryan."

Before Craig could move, Bill rose from his chair and stood rigidly, tapping his fingers on the desk as he was caught in thought. From his breast pocket he yanked out a mechanical pen, jotting down a number on a small card, the cigar in his mouth.

"Here…Dial the above if you want to reach me at home. I don't usually give it out. Oh… and before I forget, the tracking device in your head has been permanently deactivated. I know I can trust you."

They shook hands, exchanging strong eye contact. Craig walked out, passing through the hall. It was buzzing with murmuring echoes, alive with moving shadows. As he exited the building, he strolled through the car park over to his rain-dripping hover-bike.

Gripping the controls, he glided away through the city, hunger gnawing inside him; an avid hunger. He saw a snack bar; he smelt the aroma of warm coffee… He passed by but didn't stop. Ahead he heard the sound of machinery in motion; a long robot truck rumbled by, collecting scattered debris, cleaning city roads greedily. A crew of robot workmen in their dirt-ridden coveralls had started street repairs; the racket from their hammers and turbo drills was deafening. People and sounds filled virtually every corner, cries of feverish human activity. After some time he grew restless.

Pulling over, he slid to a smooth halt behind a green delivery vehicle. A uniformed driver sat, his window half-opened, nodding his head to the sound of music and words uttered. As Craig leapt from his hover-bike, he made his way into a snack-bar. People stood around eating and drinking, mouths gaping in discussion. On one side, a group of dapper city workers sat smoking, gesturing; sipping their small mugs of mint aromatic coffee, cups rattling against the saucers. In the background music was playing faintly, yet clearly audible. Steadily, he made his way to the counter. A whole selection of numbered Middle Eastern delicacies lay in front of him. He waited his turn impatiently as others were served. Then a low-pitched voice caught his attention.

"Can I help you, Sir?" a young brunette woman said, smiling behind the counter; slim and attractive, dimpled cheeks and big blue eyes. From her accent he assumed she was of Slavic descent.

"Number 20 please – oh, and a beer."

"You're not from around here, are you Sir?" the woman muttered with a self-satisfied calmness in her voice.

"What makes you think that?" he replied.

"Not quite sure...just something... Don't worry, it's a compliment."

He smiled back and without any further dialogue searched his pocket, removing loose change. Grabbing the tray of food, he moved over to the back of the elegant bar, then sat at a shiny glass table. He ate with ravished hunger, and then poured it down with his cold beer. Craig gazed for a time absently at the bustling waitresses, rapping a coin against the table in thought, everything passing in a blur.

Then he noticed a group of people looking over at him, whispers and comments exchanged under their breaths, a buzz of resentment. He calculated mentally, wondering why... The warm cosy atmosphere now began to fade. He felt alone and secluded. Lifting himself from the chair, he gently pushed his way through the throng of people hunched over, his hands thrust deep in his pockets; it was getting to be busy.

As the day flew by, nightfall was descending rapidly. In the shimmering evening twilight Craig was now on his way to the set meeting. Riding past the police headquarters, he was captivated by its elaborate design; it stood out in the city, towering high. Stationed above was a hover-port, air-vehicles ascending and descending in continual motion. He rode on through the thickening darkness, calm and focused.

In the offices of New Tec Robotics, Professor Kim Maitao sat gazing through the open balcony window at the dim stars and faint nocturnal swath of haze. Across his desk loose papers rustled as the overhead fan vented the room. Pinned and set across the walls were a series of detailed anatomy charts of the newly designed Androids, the latest in biomechanics. The buzz from his intercom speaker broke the silence; a husky yet controlled masculine voice spoke out.

"Sir, De Lucas is now here to see you."

He glanced at his pocket watch, scratching his head reflectively. The watch dials semaphored seven twenty.

"Okay, Brandon...escort him through," he replied with his sharp distinctive broken accent, his speech slightly rushed.

Sipping his glass of chilled tonic, he shuffled to his feet with expectancy. Calmly he adjusted his collar and diamond-patterned necktie, then from across his desk he released a switch. The electric powered doors opened swiftly; his eyes flickered. A shadow emerged; Craig walked in, his brown jacket hanging across his shoulder. Moving over, Kim greeted him in a professional manner.

"Professor Craig De Lucas...Kim Maitao, it's nice to meet you. Please take a seat."

Silently Craig dropped into a swivel chair facing the desk. He paused momentarily as if he was contemplating a reply.

"I trust you had a pleasant journey. When did you arrive on Earth?"

"Last night. Mind if I smoke...?"

"No, not at all. Look, I'm sorry, I know that your time spent on Mars wasn't for a recreational visit... I heard all about it."

Pulling out a cigarette from the pack, Craig lit up, puffing away without a reply, a nimbus of grey smoke circling above his head. Kim sat folding his arms, his eyes glowing in the half-light of the room. Outside there was a cracking sound of distant thunder.

"Craig, I presume you've been given a run-down in regards to this meeting?"

"Briefly; I have an idea."

"Good."

Kim straightened himself. Grabbing his drink, he gulped it down. Then from his desk drawer he pulled out a large file, placing it in front of Craig.

"Please; it's for you, an introduction... Take a look. Ten years ago this would have been unimaginable, a concept which the human mind couldn't even begin to fathom, but it's a reality...as we speak..."

Holding the file with absorbed attention, Craig flicked through the detailed papers with a fixated curiosity. Analysing the data, his eyes wondered somewhat incredulously. Then with a brisk motion, he dropped the file into his lap.

"It's quite extraordinary what you have created, Professor... The file seems to contain all the scientific and technical information in regards to how they were made. But my job is one, to create a human-friendly virus which will wipe out every living Android. What information can you supply me with in this meeting which will aid my research?"

"Our meeting here was for you to gain a deeper understanding of what you are up against. The file I have supplied you with contains all the biological data you need, but

then the rest is up to you. *Allow me to enlighten you so that you fully comprehend why we originally built these Androids...*"

Under his desk he spun a dial. Instantly a hologram ballooned into existence, the edges fading into obscurity.

"*Keep your eyes on this.*"

Three-dimensional images were displayed in an oscillating haze; images of Androids and how they were constructed, lab-grown human organs mixed with wiring and highly advanced circuit boards.

He increased the magnification until the hologram grew larger. With the spinning motion of a dial it faded with immediate effect.

"*In the last two years we have created an Android, an organic robot so human-like that you couldn't tell the difference between the two on a physiological basis; only that the Android is stronger and more advanced... It's even able to repair itself, performing the most complex tasks... From a tiny chip implanted into the cerebral cortex, we have created a virtual being to live and respond like any other ordinary human. They have emotions, a desire to eat and quench their thirst, a will and a drive to achieve and be; they are sensitive to sounds and colours, beautiful aromas; a highly developed aesthetic awareness - it's simply amazing. The very first robots that we had made were manipulated to function according to a set of laws and rules responding to programmed commands; beyond that they would simply deactivate. A matrix was responsible for regulating their thought patterns, actions and emotions...a grid screen, to be exact. The new ones are far more advanced...a startling contrast.*"

"*So why did you and your company build them?*" Craig asked, stubbing out his cigarette into an ashtray across the desk.

"*Two motives: Firstly, it was a unilateral decision between New Tec and the government. The government sponsored the project, providing all the necessary funds. Motives are as follows...for them to work with mankind and help us develop our planet, along with all the other colonised planets and space cities. Our vision of the future was this; humans and Androids together engaging in the control of the cosmos... the government felt it was essential...*"

"*Why?*"

"*You have no idea of the chaos and minefields that would have prevailed had we left the cosmos solely under the control and surveillance of human hands. Man simply hasn't got the stamina or faculty to continue managing this complex modern world alone without the aid of machines; highly advanced machines. They have given us an injection of energy, helping us to undertake some deadly and complex tasks...ones that we humans couldn't have achieved alone. For example, some of the government projects were to construct bigger space cities. Sending humans to other planets was becoming harder; it required larger amounts of money and careful planning in order to combat the dangers and hazards of the Alien worlds... The physical demands were too exacting, to say the least, on the human body; also taking into account that it was for long extended periods of time.*

"Our biggest problem was the exposure to cosmic radiation and the physiological effects that came with it... It wasn't easy for the human body to adapt to such hostile environments without there being biological changes; genetic mutations which ultimately prove fatal. Hence, sending Androids eradicated these problems. Secondly, Androids work better; quicker, more efficiently. They can construct elaborate cities, undertake deadly tasks without emotional interruption and absorb data with mind-blowing speed. In fact, recently it was discovered that they are better working and communicating with children. We had organised a series of tests at a local school. They were able to teach and instruct them in accordance to a rational technique, testing their capacities, abilities and interests. It was as if they had developed their own methodology for dealing with the children. Androids are able to perform a task, like teaching, without allowing their sentiments to deflect them in any way. Humans, on the other hand, have highly developed emotions, and are subject to chaotic chemical changes; hormonal biological activities, which in turn effect performance. The benefits that came with building these Androids were endless."

"Yes, but you obviously didn't evaluate all the possible risks. It appears you have stepped beyond your jurisdiction..."

"Craig, they were built with the best of intentions. We never expected such an attack...Our prognosis was that it would all run smoothly. As a whole, Androids are living in harmony and equality with man...but for a few who believe they should take over; they want total control and power. They have been killing humans; the list includes government officials, policemen and employees of this Corporation. I fear the numbers could grow...it could get out of hand. This is why the government needed to deploy a way to wipe them out. I provided the way...a virus is the easiest and only solution...to wage war on them would be asking for serious trouble."

Craig stood, slipping into his brown leather jacket.

"This is going to be quite a challenge for you, Craig..."

"Yes, I know...Thanks for your time. We'll be in touch."

"Naturally," he replied faintly.

Craig reached out his moist palm, and they shook hands. Silently, with a brisk action, he headed for the door. As he left the building he emerged onto the dark street. Instantly he jumped onto his hover-bike and sped away, darting through the city, street lights flashing by him in a blur as he accelerated.

Rain began to fall onto the busy metropolis of downtown Los Angeles, drenching the city with torrents of hot moisture. The city was densely populated; there had been a huge influx of a multitude of cultures, predominantly from Asian and Middle Eastern stock. Activating the rain shield, he checked his wristwatch, its green luminous dials shining in the gloom. From his intercom receptor there was a sound, a faint distant crackling sound. Across the screen a face formed in ripples of visual static... It gave out a hum as it cleared.

"Craig... Hello, can you hear me...?"

Overhead, a hover-car swept by, exceeding its legal velocity. It disappeared beyond the glowing metropolis.

"Not quite, poor reception..."

"It's me; Fred Burton. Where are you?"

"Just finished the meeting at New Tec, I'm heading home."

"Bill wanted me to call you to make sure everything was going okay."

"Yes, everything's fine..."

"Good...Mind how you go."

The line broke off abruptly; the image dimmed, wavering and fading until the screen went blank. In the distance was the Arab district of LA, an aroma of enchanting incense burning in the clammy air. Large illuminating buildings lay either side of the road, advertisement boards and street lamps flickering feebly in the gloomy haze of the city. Endless people walked by in a flurry of activity, cafes and bars scattered around. He adjusted the speed dial, lowering the velocity to almost zero.

As he pulled into a drive-through snack-bar, he came to a halt, clouds of vapour rising around him. The bar window opened. A sturdy-looking man emerged swinging a menu card towards him, his bright yellow apron fitting tightly around his torso.

"Welcome, Sir," he muttered with his noticeable hard accent, his teeth yellow and stained, his heavy beard covering his face.

"What can I get you?"

"A can of beer," he replied with distraction, his mind preoccupied with matters of cosmological importance.

Handing him a five-dollar coin, he took his ice-cold beer. Behind, a cute blonde waitress stood staring and blushing, her keen, faded green eyes wide and attractive. He lit a cigarette and sat puffing away, contemplating his lengthy discussion with Kim, recollecting all the words and data he had digested in those few hours of dialogue back at the office. Across the street he suddenly noticed a group of police troopers blending in with the forming crowds, the bar lights flickering a pale green illumination over them, unveiling certain distinctive features. There was something unusual about them; it vaguely alarmed him. He looked on curiously. They appeared inquisitive; bits of muffled conversation drifted to him. He began to suspect they were Androids. On the surface they appeared organic, but they moved somewhat mechanically. Rapidly he dismissed the possibility; after all, it was against government regulations. As he gulped down the remainder of his chilled beer, he dropped his cigarette to the ground, grinding it underfoot. He wiped his mouth, catching his breath, and then tossed the empty can into a nearby bin; with it, the day's anxieties.

Hurriedly he made his way home, passing through the city. On one side of the road a holographic advertisement flashed into life. 'New Space City Apartments available.' Sharp pictures followed. It was now common for humans to live in space cities; gigantic spheres constructed from complex alloys able to accommodate millions of people in an indoor world, Earth-like. The spinning effect simulated a gravity field in which human life was sustainable, along with a magnetic field which repelled hazardous energetic particles, lethal cosmic radiation. Entering his now-familiar luxury downtown apartment, it was dark and silent, the shades half pulled across a large window overlooking the city. With the command of his voice the lights activated. In brisk motion the automatic vent switched on, humming air around the room. In the corner the vision set was playing, broadcasting the night news. The volume rose until it was audible.

Walking to the bar he poured a double shot of Jim Beam. He sat on his light green sofa straining it down slowly; he began to relax, sinking into its comfy cushions, his supple arm thrown lightly over the back. On the wall was a glass-framed collection of worms finely pressed into cotton; Martian life forms, to be exact, which had been collected and smuggled to Earth from Mars. It evoked unwanted memories. They were dead of course, unable to survive the Earth's heavy atmosphere. His eyes grew tired, his mind wandering as he looked apathetically at the collection. Then from across the table he began consulting his notes. At that moment there was a sound of rustling footsteps. He paused.

"Bill, is that you?"

There was no reply. Placing his glass down, he remained still. A sharp knock followed. Rising to his feet, he walked to the door. He could hear the sound of panting. From the security monitor he saw Bill Ryan.

Briskly, he opened. Bill stood there dejected, feet wide apart, his pinstripe suit ripped, his face the manifestation of terror. Falling to the ground, Craig reached out his hands and held him, supporting him into the room.

"*What the hell happened?*"

He moved to the bar, pouring him a glass of soda. Staggering to the couch, Bill sat, his face flushed with panic, his chest rising and falling as he panted uncontrollably. His body sagged, his lips and hands twitching nervously.

"*We've got to get away!*"

Craig stopped his features twisting into a frown of panic. Hurriedly, he moved over, kneeling by his side.

"*Why...? What do you mean...? Tell me, what happened to you?*"

Bill looked up. He took a deep breath and exhaled, attempting to regain his composure.

"*Craig, the Androids... They've infiltrated the police force...the government... Quick, we've got to get out of here before they find us... They tried to kill me... Fred Burton is one of them.*"

His voice wavered and faded.

"*They are in control... We can't trust anyone, do you hear? No one... You've got to shut down the sphere...*"

For a second he lost his wording. Craig caught the intense appeal and desperation in his voice. He inched closer as Bill began to whisper in his ear with straining effort......

"*The sphere... you've got to locate it...*"

Before he could speak any further there was a tapping sound at the door, then a moment of static and silence.

"*Wait, don't open,*" Bill gasped, his hands shaking as he half rose from the chair, refraining from an impulsive reaction.

From under the couch Craig pulled out his powerful handgun. Moving to the door, he glanced at the security monitor. There was no one.

Then the monitor went blank. Suddenly, the door blew apart. A deep rolling wave of force rippled through the apartment; the ground heaved and shook with it. At once Craig flew back with the force of the blast, crashing to the ground. A numbing pain swept through him, pain then rolling clouds of blackness. He lay still, dazed and unaware.

Across the room loose pieces of wood and shrapnel flung against the walls violently in all directions; glass from a large hanging mirror smashing, raining down with a racket of shivering fragments. Smoke filled the room; particles of grey ash and dust rising, licking crackles of fire.

Through the dense smoke two men emerged dressed in black suits, blast pistols in their hands waist-high. Reaching for his handgun, Bill was shot in the chest, a string of glowing yellow laser beams piercing through him like a searing line of heat. He lay on the couch lifeless, arms flung wide apart.

As Craig regained consciousness, he grabbed his gun, scrambling wildly to his feet. Almost losing his footing he stumbled towards the backroom, feeling his way through blindly, sweat and blood trickling down his cheeks, streaked across his collar. The thin acrid smell of the blast made his eyes water. He coughed weakly, clearing his lungs.

Concealing himself behind a mirrored closet, he gripped the handgun firmly, his finger on the trigger. Cold fear threatened to overwhelm him. He waited, calculating pensively. He heard footsteps and then silence, the floorboards creaking eerily. Suddenly there was a stir of motion. Across the ground he saw shadows as the two men entered the room. Leaping out, he fired repeatedly. His body jerked back as the gun sounded with deafening shrills. In a flash it was over. It went quiet; his adrenal fix began to decrease. The two men lay on the ground, eyes and mouth flung open and dead, curls of smoke pouring out from their chests. Sparks began to shower the room, darting out from the gaping bullet holes, the cords in their necks flexing furiously, ceasing moments later. Cautiously, he moved over, gradual comprehension coming to him; his heart hammering wildly, nervous sweat oozing from his pores. An odour of burning metal filled the air, sharp and toxic. Craig shuddered and coughed.

Kneeling down, he realised with instant shock they were Androids. A maze of wiring and circuitry was clearly visible, a glint of metal too. On the ground was a soggy mass of grey coloured matter. In their jacket pockets he found two ID cards; both were registered as detectives. He paused in terror. Searching on, he found a brown wallet. He removed the contents, flicking through carefully; money, receipts then a card: 'Chows Wine bar'. Dropping the wallet absently, he rushed over to Bill through a haze of rising smoke and dust, shards of broken glass and debris crunching under his feet. He checked for a pulse; there was nothing.

From the window he saw a number of air-vehicles approaching in the distance. From their distinctive shape and design he was certain they were police troopers. Then the sound of sirens followed; his suspicion was now confirmed - he had no choice but to run. Overcome with panic, he fled through the hallway, sprinting in the direction of the elevator. On the way he almost collided with a frightened old man as he came out from his room shaking and concerned, his glasses hanging from one ear. *"Hey, what's happening?"* he yelled at the top of his voice with cold twisting terror. Jabbing the elevator button, the doors slid back; Craig was now away. Reaching ground level, he raced through the lobby doors out into the night darkness, his body leaning forward. Hastily he jumped onto his hover-bike, setting it in motion. He halted, breathing deeply, trying to orientate himself as the dim gleam of the half-moon shone down over him.

Within minutes he had left the scene, gliding through LA. His body ached, his ears ringing. Even his eyes were blurred, burning with dust fragments due to the blast. Ahead he noticed a team of police vehicles heading in his direction. He looked again through the blurring rain. In an instant he turned into a side road and parked up. People were moving by in their countless hundreds; a seething mass of confusion, night clubs and blazing music. He gazed around, contemplating. In the rainy gloom he saw the blue lights of a bar.

With calmed urgency he jumped off and made his way through the heavy plush doors, wiping sweat and stained blood from his upper lip. People began to turn and stare inquisitively; others gave the odd backward glance. At that moment he felt a wave of dizziness. Blackness swirled around him; it passed almost as quickly as it had come. He looked around the dimly lit bar, shifting colour floor lights winking on and off in the amber gloom. People stood sipping cocktails, laughing and discussing, their mouths gaping, mumbling meaningless sounds, heads and arms moving energetically to the chords of exotic Middle-Eastern music. Overhead, hanging in wire brass cages, were a variety of mechanical birds, multi-coloured, used as part of the bar's décor. Squeezing his way through a surging mass of people, he noticed his old friend Ben, a misty layer of cigarette smoke clouding his vision and commingling with the dull stench of alcohol. Hurriedly, Craig approached him. He turned, his eyes igniting with excited alarm.

"Hey, Craig, you're back…What happened?"

"Ben, we need to speak… I need your help…"

"Hey, steady…what's going on? Tell me, what is it?" he asked, eagerly awaiting a reply.

Craig swallowed hard, his face contorted with sadness. He looked helplessly about the bar, gazing at the sea of faces, his shoulders sagging. With the stare of his eyes, he signalled his frustration…

"It's complicated... Can we go somewhere?"

Ben's sparkling personality seemed to dissolve as he stood there momentarily lost for words. After an interval of hesitation he went to reply. At that moment a waiter pushed between them holding a tray of drinks, almost losing his footing. The music began to rise. An excited murmur swept through the crowd.

"Come, let's get out of here." Ben said firmly.

Back at Ben's house, Craig had been explaining all the unfolding events.

He paced around the room anxiously, clasping and wringing his hands in a torment of incomprehension. Ben sat back against his cream white sofa, magazines and papers on its arms. He listened intently, his feet resting on a blond oak table, his eyes alight with unquenchable horror. Licking his lips piteously, he remained hushed.

"...He also mentioned something about a sphere...before he could finish, they broke in and killed him... I'm not quite sure what he was trying to tell me..."

Craig paused, gazing at Ben, somewhat confounded by his unquestioning reaction. He began to chew and bite into his lip, and frown in thought. Abruptly Ben replied, leaning forward.

"Look...all of this doesn't come as a surprise to me...I've known this for quite some time... Maybe not to this extent. In fact, a close friend of mine has been revealing some starling things..."

The tension in his voice was noticeable.

"What things?"

"She believes she's found the way to stop them, the only way...but she still hasn't disclosed it to me yet. It could well be a virus, but I'm not certain. I'm seeing her tomorrow... In fact, you met her on several occasions; Connie Rodgers, she works as my assistant down at the forensic Laboratories..."

"Yes... I remember her well..."

Craig reflected, moodily shaking his head. He groped in his pocket, pulling out a tube of narcotic headache pills. Pulling off the lid, he placed two pills into his mouth and swallowed. Then, moving to the window, he looked out. A portion of the night sky opened up through growing cloud formations, a distinctive glaze of luminous stars gleaming faintly. He stood there contemplating, his eyes slanting with fatigue. Ben sat absorbed in mutual thought. They continued in silence for a while.

"Look, Craig, I think we should get some rest... In the morning I'll contact Connie... You can take the guest room down the hall."

"Thanks. I feel totally exhausted... but I think I'll be okay here on the sofa."

"Okay, that's fine. If you need food or drink, help yourself."
Calmly, Ben made his way to bed, the night drifting by in a flash.
In the morning clouds covered the skyline and beyond, cancelling the sun's rays. A torrent of rain hammered down, hot moisture rising in the atmosphere. Outside, the city was a beehive of activity, air and surface vehicles moving in all directions. From the sofa Craig awoke, clearing his eyes after some much-needed sleep, a feeling of uncertainty and dread clouding his tortured mind. Moving to the bathroom, he opened the taps, filling the basin with warm water, steaming up the mirror with moisture. His mouth was cut, caked with dried blood. In the background he heard the morning paper land on the porch. Washing his face down with soapy water, he dried himself and then made his way to the door; standing there was Ben, slipping into a silk white shirt, tucking it into his faded black jeans.
"I spoke to Connie. She's waiting for us…"
"Now?"
"Whenever you're ready…"
Walking back into the living room, Craig seated himself, tossing the towel onto the table. He put on his shoes and then pulled on his shirt. Through the drapes shone a ray of yellow sunlight breaking through the rainy clouds, beating down against the tiled floor. Ben walked in, grabbing his white jacket from across the sofa.
As midday approached they drove through the city, Craig lying back pondering pensively, Ben tuning into the morning news. On either side of the road were towering skyscrapers, robot traffic wardens roaming the streets, hover-cars and bikes moving around in a circuitry of motion.
Pulling into a side road, Ben parked up, coasting to a halt. A gang of youths walked by smoking cigarette pipes. The road was littered with scattered debris, empty beer cans, cigarette butts and papers. The doors opened; they moved out, heading in the direction of a huge apartment block. From the distance there was the sound of a passing hover-train. Across the street, in the form of a holograph projection, was an advertisement displaying a list of jobs for humans. 'Performers Wanted, Dancers and Singers.'
As they reached the apartment block, Ben pressed the buzzer, sliding back his thin black hair. A face formed on the vid-screen.
"Hi, Connie…."
Instantly the glass doors opened with a click.

Reaching the tenth floor, they walked to her apartment. As they approached, Connie came out, her long dark hair hanging raggedly across her gaunt face, her limbs slender and supple, fresh excited tears welling in her blue eyes. On her wrists were two brown coloured bands, almost matching the rich bronze hue of her skin.

"Craig, it's good to see you! It's been so long... Ben explained everything to me this morning... Come, we've got to talk."

As they entered, she moved to the window, opening the heavy drapes; daylight instantly filtered through. Before them stood a fireplace, where a raging synthetic fire blazed. No heat was dispersed; it was there purely as part of the décor. The room was warm and inviting, filled with oil paintings and antique artefacts from distant continents. The sparkling marble floor was decorated with an elaborate pattern, the walls painted ecru. In the corner the vision set was playing with muted volume.

"Did you make sure no one was following you here?"

"No, Connie, don't worry," Ben replied.

"I'm sorry, I'm just so nervous; I don't know what to expect."

Gently she sat, crossing her legs, smoothing down her skirt around her shapely thighs. Craig walked over and sat beside her. She looked up, beaming at him warmly, her lashes flickering modestly.

"Well, Connie... Tell me all you know."

His face was set with stern concentration. She cleared her throat and began explaining.

"A friend of mine - Jim Corrigan, a retired worker at New Tec - alerted me as to what was transpiring... He recently discovered that the Androids can be stopped... not by means of a virus but by detecting and locating the life source sphere and shutting it down. The sphere is what keeps these Androids alive. It needs to be deactivated - once deactivated, the code signal will be broken."

A chilling premonition swept over him. He calculated mentally, a mass of ideas brilliantly lighting his mind. He raised his hand with animation, and then banged his fist against the arm of the sofa.

"That's what Bill meant...That's what he was trying to tell me. Damn, this means the company that built them must be in on it. New Tec have no intention of stopping the Androids. Obviously, Professor Maitao is behind it all... He misled us..."

"Exactly."

"Why didn't Jim alert the government from the onset?"

"The day he found out, he went missing - four days back. My conversation with him was probably my last; we had organised to meet in the evening at my apartment, but he never showed... Haven't heard a word since."

"We need to alert the government authorities immediately - at least, the humans!"

"No, I don't think that's a good idea," she replied, her voice now grated with anguish and pent-up anxiety. *"It's pointless and highly dangerous; they will never believe us. They trust New Tec; they will never accept that they are behind it - especially coming from you. Besides, you need to keep a low profile; the police probably want you for questioning in regard to the shootout... And as things look, half the police force is probably under their control. They use their incredible human appearance to their advantage - it will be too dangerous."*

"What do you mean?" Craig said, frantic thoughts whizzing through his mind.

"Jim told me he believed many of them had illegally taken hold of fake human identification cards which allowed them to undertake government positions - positions within the police force. Posing as humans is their biggest weapon... It's so hard to tell the difference between a human and an Android. The government had initially devised a way, an A-TEST, but it proved to be totally inaccurate. Besides that, Jim reckoned they could replicate themselves; hence, the number of government registered Androids is probably inaccurate. Who knows how many there are, if true. We have to locate the life sphere ourselves and shut it down; it's the only solution."

"Tell me, did Jim mention where it's located?"

"No, but I would imagine that it's within the building at New Tec, perhaps in a secret underground lab. If we go to Jim's apartment, we might find some vital information that could lead us to it..."

Gracefully, Connie slid out a silver disc from her blouse, and then placed it into Craig's hand.

"Here...This key will get us in. I was too frightened to go there alone. We'll wait till nightfall - it will be safer."

The day slipped by, the half-hidden sun slowly vanishing into the horizon, darkness breaking into the fading light. Before long, the sky was pitch-black and overcast. Craig sat rolling and crumpling a piece of torn paper in his hands pensively, Connie and Ben sound asleep. Suddenly the vid-phone buzzed; they awoke with startled, questioning eyes. Hurrying over, Connie answered.

"Hello...?"

There was no reply; the line went dead, followed by static. Craig raced over, gripping the vid-phone from the clutch of her slender hands. As he went to listen in, he heard some movement from beyond the front door.

He stood still…dead still, strange emotions twisting through him. Dropping the vid-phone vacantly, he pulled out his gun.

"Someone's there!"

Again, there was the sound of motion. As he moved to the door, he gripped the handle, swinging it open. He leapt out, clenching the gun with both hands. The hallway was bare. His eyes flashed suspiciously, his heart beating with vigour. Ben came out from the apartment, walking towards him, hushed as he looked around.

"Quick! We can't chance it, we've got to get out of here," Craig said.

Ben turned sharply, moving back into the room, his eyes ablaze with determination.

"Connie, we've got to leave now… Hurry!"

Slipping into her fluffy white coat, her breathing grew heavy and erratic. Behind, Craig rushed in. At that moment the lights flickered and dimmed; the room then plunged into complete darkness. The entire building had lost all electrical power; it was dark everywhere. Above, there were groans, voices rising; a muffled concoction of distorted sounds coming from the neighbouring apartments. The groans grew. From the hallway, emergency lights activated, strong and luminous.

As they dashed out, an Android was advancing from beyond the winding hallway, dressed in a grey coloured suit. In its hand it held a large blast pistol, loaded and ready to fire. From the Android's eyes shone a brilliant fiery light, almost consuming; its face was butch and stern, devoid of human emotion. Dropping to the ground, Craig pulled the trigger repeatedly, firing at it with furious effort, halting it and bursting it into parts. The laser tube, which it carried internally, bounced and rolled on the ground, echoing and diminishing into nullification. There was an astonished silence. As the smoky haze from the blasts faded, he looked on…

Unbelievably, he noticed signs of life; its arms moving in convulsions, flicking and twitching. Sparks began to spew out from its gaping mouth; there was a stench of burning metal and wire. Craig cleansed sweat from his bloodshot eyes as he panted. He rose swiftly to his feet, looking behind. He saw an exit for the stairway, a glowing green sign.

"Hurry, down there!"

Running on, there was gunfire. Ben was shot and with immediate effect dissolved into particles, his car-activator disc lying on the ground. Gripped with cold twisting terror, Connie looked back, the colour draining from her face. Craig, pulling at her coat, constrained his emotions, his fingers digging in and tightening.

"We've got to keep moving!" he cried out, almost demanding.

From the floor he picked up the car-disc. Behind he heard heavy footsteps as the Android rose to its feet, swaying back and forth, its face set with grim determination, its body half-blown apart. Then with lighting speed it fired; a laser beam passed narrowly above Craig's head, a rolling wave of heat penetrating into the wall with a vicious bang.

A portion of the wall was now missing; the air was full of the blast smell, a bitter choking stench. With the force of his leg, Craig shoved the door open, holding her by the hand. Rapidly they made their way down a twisting flight of stairs. Within a short period they had reached the ground floor beside the exit, a curl of loose wallpaper flapping as air currents seeped through an opened window. Outside in the sky, he noticed a police-air-vehicle gliding in the atmosphere. Slowly it polarised into position, descending towards the ground, almost disappearing into the surging rain. Sliding the door open, they dashed over towards the hover-car, hurrying across the busy city through dense traffic. Curious faces turned, devoid of expression. A taxi swerved and halted abruptly.

"Hey, watch where you're going…!"

He flung out his fist, waving it in anger. Reaching the hover-car, Craig opened the doors. They sat; a gush of cool air blew in, and with it city fumes and smog. Connie looked back, her face tight with tension, her jaw locked rigidly. Craig snapped on the power and backed out onto the main road, luminous dials swinging into activity. During a break in the traffic he sped away, increasing the power of the headlights, his face pale and grim.

Gripping the wheel with numb hands, he guided the hover-car expertly, tires splashing through the drenched city road with fury, streets and signs flashing past. A few metres ahead the traffic lights turned red; a crowd of people walked by holding large umbrellas shielding themselves from the relentless rain. Their footsteps rang out against the pavement as they hurriedly moved along. Squeezing the brake pedal, the hover-car came to a halt. Craig was silent. He reached over, stroking her leg.

"What now, Craig?" she gasped. Her eyes fixed at him intently, peering into his depths.

"Let's get out of here; then we'll talk." He held her slender hand with a secure grip, as if transmitting courage into her.

The lights turned green; they moved away, heading to the outskirts of the city towards the coast, a good forty-minute drive.

Parked on a dirt track in a corner of a deserted road they sat, a dull droning sound echoing from a nearby factory, a range of ragged hills jutted ahead in the distance in the violet gloom. A passing spacecraft roared by, shattering the evening silence. The wind began to gain speed, surging against the trees like a raging tide, insistent and powerful, whipping the foul-smelling mists into the night air.

Above, dense red clouds separated, unveiling a few distant stars; space without depth. Connie turned, looking over towards him, the sad glow of defeat in her eyes. She tried to repress the impulse to cry but it proved too much.

"I can't believe it… I can't believe what's happening…"

She broke down, her eyes swelling with unwanted tears, tears burning in her eyes. Craig reached over and embraced her, holding her tight, his fingers running through her hair. With a feeble, broken voice she spoke out.

"There's nowhere left to run…"

Craig pulled away, looking out into the darkness, into the void, towards the distant range of hills, the wind and rain surging on.

"Connie, you've got to be strong. We must locate the sphere before they find us…you must remain calm and see it through."

She nodded absently, taking a shuddering deep breath, trying to focus her mind.

At midnight they were back in the city, east of Los Angeles, parked outside Jim's apartment building in the quiet suburban area of Pasadena. It was covered in lavish apartments and immense parks. Stepping out of the hover-car, Craig stood for a brief time taking in the scene. With his lighter he lit a cigarette and headed through the plush open apartment doors. Inside the lobby was a flowing fountain, bright flickering lights around its gold rim. It was filled with colourful corals, mixed with an array of exotic fish swimming in crystal clear water.

Calling the elevator, they entered, ascending towards the fiftieth floor; it moved rapidly with a faint hum. Craig stood there puffing away in deep thought. Leaning back, Connie held her head; a quiet dejected figure of a woman. In her mind she could see vivid images of Ben, now no longer there, the Android gunning him down. It was playing over and over in her tortured mind. Within a matter of seconds the elevator doors opened. Cautiously, Craig walked out. The hallway lights activated; he looked either side. It was silent; even the rustling of human activity was lacking. Quietly, they began to make their way down, eyes roaming alertly. Then a tall light-haired Teutonic-looking woman walked out from one of the apartments at the far end of the hall, a synthetic tobacco cigarette sloping from her mouth, red lipstick sealed across her lips. Her fingers were slender and exquisitely tapered. The rich aroma of perfumed smoke filled the corridor, drifting out through an opened window into the void. She passed by in a hurry, scrambling out a neck scarf from her brown leather bag.

Then she stopped at the elevators, dropping her cigarette on the marble floor and grinding it down with her heel. The elevator opened; she moved on. Walking to Jim's apartment, Craig quietly deactivated the lock at the door with the disc. A green light shone from the disc-slot. He halted, swallowing nervously, and then slowly pushed the door open. As they entered, it was unusually warm. At the far side of the room stood a long Romanesque pillar; placed above was a globe-shaped ornament, a captivating globe of colours. Other fanciful artefacts stood out in the luscious apartment; statues and sculptures, elaborate furniture; everything seemed to sparkle. Closing the door shut, he stood still, his eyes roaming actively. In the corner, resting against a wooden stool, he noticed a wet umbrella, a raincoat folded neatly beside it. Across the tiled floor were fresh dirt footprints. Kneeling down, he examined the mud prints. Indeed, they were fresh. He rubbed his fingers in the dirt, then stood up pensively.

"Someone's been here today. Maybe we missed them by minutes!"

"Nobody but me has access to this place - at least, not to my knowledge..."

"Whoever came here needed no invitation."

The atmosphere in the room became stiff and uncomfortable; even the air seemed to have its own mysterious scent to it. Without a word he turned, glancing around uneasily. Walking over to the table, he stubbed out his cigarette into a glass ashtray. As he went to move away he noticed a piece of gum pressed against the table; it was moist, wet with saliva. Calmly he headed into the bedroom and began searching, scanning the room vigilantly. He yanked open drawers and cabinets, spilling their contents onto the floor; he checked behind chairs and tables but found nothing - at least, nothing of any relevance. From under the bed he slid out a box filled with a wide spectrum of herbal remedies, a whole mixture of Far Eastern medicines.

Exiting the bedroom, he searched on restlessly. In a drawer located in the front room he found an Electromagnetic acoustic transducer. He emptied out the remainder of the contents, working feverishly with frantic haste. Finally he found a small book; a diary. He leant down and opened it at random, holding together a few loose pages, Connie inching her way over curiously. Expertly he leafed through, his mind set and focused, blank page after blank page. Then he found a list of appointments; various times, various destinations, a list of names, then a photo - a picture of Jim.

Holding it for a time, he then dropped it to the floor. Connie stood there, static and silent, her smudged eyeliner darkening her saddened eyes. Suddenly there was a sound coming from the kitchen. He drew his gun and aimed. A shadow emerged - a small grey cat walked out, cute and fluffy; it purred and rolled around the floor in search of attention. Craig stood relieved, lowering his gun; he took a breath and exhaled. From its loose hanging tail, it was dead obvious to him that it was a mechanical pet; red and green wires were clearly visible.

"What now, Craig? We've found nothing."

He turned and reached over to her, gazing at her fragile frame and innocent eyes with compassion and sincerity, yet amidst the cocktail of emotions he could not ignore the flutters of love. The chemistry was there. Gently, he pulled away, repressing his natural impulses; her breath, eager and erratic, tickled his neck.

"Let's give it a few more minutes... We're bound to find something."

Moving towards a desk he noticed a glass ball atlas; instinctively and without thought he began spinning it. Unexpectedly, from the floor a secret compartment opened before him, a gaping hole. A loaded gun lay there. He knelt down and looked in.

"There's nothing here - just a gun. I guess that's it... We've no choice but to go to NEW TEC and find it... The sphere has to be there somewhere. It's time to pay Professor Maitao a visit."

"How do you plan on getting in? It won't be easy."

"No, it won't. But don't worry, I'll find a way. We'll head there at sunrise, map out a route in, and then execute it come nightfall."

Walking out, they left the building, heading for the hover-car.

Morning approached; sunlight streamed down between broken clouds, filtering through an avenue of trees. It sparkled for a time, shining on the bonnet, and then vanished, hidden behind dense clouds. The roads were rain drenched; vapour rising, dissipating slowly. Half dozing, Craig had spent much of the night in deep contemplation as he sat in the hover-car, Connie lying still, asleep on the passenger seat. Straightening himself, he consulted his wristwatch; it was well past 11am. He yawned, fatigue showing in his drooping shoulders. As he turned on the radio Connie awoke. She looked up, disorientated.

"What time is it?"

"11.40 am."

She cleared her eyes and stretched, adjusting herself to the early morning light. Instantly the surroundings reminded her of where she was. Swiftly, Craig began driving towards the city centre, his face alive with hope. Thirty minutes had passed; they were now near the LA hover-station. It was busy, workers rushing in and out of the glass entrance. A janitor sat washing down the steps. In front was a row of impatient taxi drivers, sitting and sweating in the humidity of the day. People rushed and moved feverishly in the boundless confusion. Myriads of inhabitants swarmed about their activities. Pulling to the side, Craig stopped the car. His head spun. Outlined against the sky was a spacecraft returning from Mars; a roaring blur of speed. He was motionless, his mind momentarily dazed, cut off from the bustle and sounds of the outside world. A sharp knock against the window alarmed him. He looked over; his heart skipped a beat...

An Android - a police trooper.

"Sorry Sir, it's a non-parking zone, you'll have to move on."

Immediately Craig recognised that it was an Android. His face was refined, well-structured; in terms of his physical appearance he appeared human, but his thin, somewhat metallic voice gave him away - obviously a defective robot. The Android grinned mechanically then turned, walking away, blending in with the busy crowds. Craig felt a rushing splurge of relief. He accelerated, driving away. After a few minutes they approached a skyscraper, huge windows reflecting the dim orb of the half-hidden sun. Connie sat up, pointing and staring.

"There...That's where I work. LA Forensic Labs."

Craig slowed down. Suddenly a rumble of frightened murmurs swept through the crowds; people were rushing, panic, chaos and confusion everywhere. From behind he heard sirens wailing; a row of police-vehicles came shooting towards them. Nervous fear swept through him like electricity. He saw a side road ahead. At once he turned, sharply swerving around the corner, accelerating away.

"Damn it... How're we doing, Connie?"

"Okay. They're out of sight…but I can still hear sirens; they must be close."

Hurriedly, he sized up the traffic pattern, cutting past oncoming vehicles in rapid succession. He looked ahead, glimpsing in the rear view mirror at sharp intervals, sweat dripping down his neck into his collar. At the end of the road he came to a junction. He moved out, blending in with the moving traffic. The rain began to ease, almost to a halt. He felt alone, entangled in a deadly spiral of cat and mouse.

Further on he noticed a police-air-vehicle gliding overhead; the traffic began to slow down to a walking pace. A team of armed police troopers suddenly emerged from beyond the streets, swarming up onto the pathway. With little option he drove towards the entrance of a huge car park, a sophisticated steel structure. Halting at the barrier, he pressed for a ticket; the barrier rose and he went through. Hover-cars and bikes filled virtually every space, but then he noticed an empty bay. Slowly he parked up, sighing with relief, the strong overhead lights beating down against the bonnet. With the look of a lost child, Connie reached over to him, resting her head on his shoulder in search of protection. He held her tightly in his arms.

"Are you okay?"

She nodded back, and replied, *"Yes…but I can't see us making it, Craig. They're on to us and they won't stop."*

"Trust me, we will. For now we'll stay put. We can't take any chances. We've got to wait till nightfall."

He broke off and sat there lapsing into silence, his eyes straying away from her. Before long he drifted into a deep sleep, hours passing, his mind engaged in vivid dreams… dreams without meaning, a confusion of senseless sounds and images flooding his mind. Then he awoke in a nervous twitch, his eyes flying open. He checked his watch; it was already 6pm. Next to him Connie sat resting. Slowly she began to open her heavy-lidded eyes.

"It's dark outside - we must have slept hours."

"Yeah…it appears so," he replied groggily.

Across the street, shop lights glowed, red and blue. He then opened the window, struggling to take in the thin weak air. Behind he heard the sound of footsteps. A car park attendant walked by dressed in a luminous yellow single-breasted jacket and faded green trousers. Slowly he began to approach the hover-car. Parting a few strands of thin wispy hair, the elderly Chinese man knelt by the door.

"I'm sorry, Sir... Just came by to check if you're okay. We've seen you and the lady lying in the car for a number of hours from our security monitor back in the control surveillance room - everything okay?"

Reluctantly, Craig replied.

"Yes, I'm okay. Thanks,"

The man rose to his feet and leisurely walked away. Again Craig checked his watch.

"It looks like it's safe to leave now. We'll head to New Tec from here."

Slowly, they made their way out of the car park into the late evening twilight. The rain began pelting down; activating the wipers, he kept his eyes sharply focused. After what seemed only a matter of minutes they were almost there; the dome-shaped structure was towering high, a dazzling neon sign ahead: 'NEW TEC ROBOTICS'. Veering the hover-car to the left, he parked up. Out in the distance, a line of trees and buildings faded into the silence and night vapours. From his jacket he pulled out his gun, clicking the safety lock into place, doubts and fear twisting through him.

"Connie, wait here..."

"Be careful, Craig," she replied. Deeply concerned, she sensed the rapid flight of his hidden thoughts; the transitions showed on his tense face and fear-glazed eyes.

Suppressing his anxieties, he smiled; a smile of complete assurance. In return she nodded absently, her eyes roaming vacantly, set with a dazed expression of uncertainty.

Pushing the door open, he stepped out onto the road, the sound of breaking raindrops diminishing as the storm began to ease. Cautiously he looked around; no one in sight apart from the occasional air and surface vehicle whizzing by. Sharply he held his watch up; the face of it was dark, malfunctioning. He brought his arm closer to his eyes and read it in the starlight. Lifting his jacket collars, he commenced a slow walk towards the building, a block away.

As he approached he looked up, assessing the situation; it wasn't going to be easy to gain entry. Two burly-looking security guards stood at the entrance smoking, dressed in their familiar blue uniforms. He pondered, ideas running through his mind. Then he noticed a delivery truck, coloured a brilliant silver, stopping at the security gate. A thought struck him.

Unhindered and without violation he dashed over, keen and ready. As the luminous barrier rose, the truck began to move through. Instantly he knelt down, sliding underneath, gripping onto all he could; twisted metal bars, pipes and links. His face was immersed in smoke, droplets of dirt and water falling into his eyes. Desperately he held on, his legs wrapped around; the straining effort on his arms was testing. Seconds later it reversed, backing up into a bay; then it juddered, coming to a halt. It all went quiet. He paused.

Loosening his grip, he lay down on the cold hard tarmac, recapturing his breath. Limply he slid out from under the truck, rising to his feet with caution. With the beating sound of footsteps, he noticed the driver walking over towards the cargo inspector. Further on he saw a wide door; an entrance point into the building. Craig remained still for a time, his eyes roaming from left to right. Then briskly he moved away, concealing himself behind a row of parked hover-cars. Directly in front, only a few metres away, he saw an office; a surveillance hut.

Rapidly he entered, dragging the door shut after him. No one was there; it was vacant. On a large desk was an open news journal filled with the world of reality; across from it, an air fan whirring. In the corner was a series of monitors, a cigarette left smouldering in an ashtray burning slowly into ash. Then he heard a noise. He turned, shifting his gaze towards a blue flashing light; a small microwave. Warm, unscented food slid out on a plate, soft chimes sounding, ceasing moments later. Before he could move, the door swung wide open. A guard walked in; a grey haired figure of a man wearing sharply pressed black trousers, a dark grey jacket fixed tightly to his body.

"*Hey, who are you...? What are you doing here? Got some ID?*" he said, tapping his mechanical pencil against his clipboard.

As Craig reached for his gun, the guard went to strike him with a clenched fist, dropping his clipboard to the ground. Craig ducked, sliding lithely aside with lightning motion. Pulling out his gun, he swung it at him, striking him on the jaw. The guard dropped to his knees, and then fell face-down as if hit with a bolt of force at the stomach. He was aware that Craig was standing over him.

"*Listen to me,*" Craig bent down, the gun pointing, his finger tightening on the trigger. "*Get me into the building... Now!*"

From his pocket the guard pulled out a swipe card with a shaky hand; an ID number lay written across it.

"*Here...*" he mumbled, his chest rising and falling with the effort of breathing; a haze of fear oozing from his stuttering voice. "*All you've got to do is swipe it through the code reader by the door.*"

Craig snatched it, his eyes briefly deflected.

"Get up, you're coming with me." His face was set with grim purpose, the cords in his hand bulging as he tightened his grip on the gun.

"How many workers in the building at present?"

"Very few; hardly any," the guard muttered weakly.

"And Professor Maitao...?"

"Yes," he hesitated, his eyes roaming. *"Yes, the Professor is in his lab."*

"Good, take me there!"

Moving out of the surveillance hut, Craig steered him to the doorway, the gun sinking into his back. Luckily, no one seemed to be looking. With the swipe card, Craig fed it through the code reader; with brisk effect the door opened. Walking in, the hallway was clear. No one in sight; nothing stirred apart from the sound of working machinery. They walked on, Craig blinking, adjusting to the dim light of the hall. Reaching the elevators, he stabbed the call button; before long they entered. Within seconds they had arrived on the tenth floor; the elevator opened. There was a cold silence, the overhead lights glowing faintly.

"Where now?"

"At the far end of the hall to the right..."

Ahead of them a thick metal door closed off the hallway. Craig walked over, attempting to open it, but it wouldn't budge. He turned, pointing the gun at the guard.

"Open it!"

The guard retreated, making no move.

"I can't... The only way to deactivate the lock is with a special entry card. Only a few people in this building have access through..."

"I'll blast it open!"

Across the guard's belt Craig noticed a set of handcuffs. Rapidly he slid them off, fastening one end across the guard's wrist; the other around a long metal pole which was connected from the ceiling to the floor - a ventilation system. The guard sat there, powerless and withdrawn.

Cautiously Craig advanced. At the door he fired repeatedly, blasting it at the lock. Reaching for the slender handle, it came off in his hand, dropping to the floor and breaking into bits. He pushed the door open. It swung and then blocked halfway; there was a sharp grinding sound of hinges. Passing through a winding hallway, he eventually reached an entrance to a laboratory. He heard a noise; a rustling of papers. With a stern shove against the door, he blasted his way in.

"Game over, Professor... Where's the life source sphere?"

There was a brief delay before the professor replied.

"Put the gun down, Craig. Don't fight what you don't understand!"

His eyes were cunning and cold, his mind shifting into a state of cognitive dissonance.

"You're insane." Stretching out his arm, he pointed the gun with precise aim, his face ablaze with rage.

"No, Craig, I'm not insane." He clenched both fists, his face now coloured in reddish anger.

"What do you propose I do, give up what I alone created? Mankind has stepped into new frontiers – revolutionary - all because of me. I have left a mark on the Earth for all to see; the greatest mark of human accomplishment to date."

"These machines are bloodthirsty... They want control. You must stop them."

"No, Craig, I refuse to undo what I created. It was never my intention for them to rise up against humans - what is happening is of no consequence to me. Humans are inferior, Craig. An Android has become the perfect instructor, well capable of replacing us and maintaining the cosmos, superior in strength and faculty - the master race. You know yourself that humans show no ability to manage a complex modern society... Is there a human capable of leading mankind?"

He stood up impetuously from his desk, his eyes set, glowing with a crazed reflected glory. There was a strange granite cast to his face, an unearthly hardness. Craig moved over, waving the snout of the gun.

"Earth belongs to us humans - there can be only one ruler. Where is the sphere? Don't let me ask you again!"

"If this is the ultimatum, then I have no choice..."

At that moment he crouched down, pulling out a slender line blast gun from his belt with lighting speed, his features twisting wildly. Before he could fire, Craig shot him repeatedly. Staggering around the room, he fought to keep his balance. Then his legs gave way, his gun swaying from his hand. With a cold hard thump he crashed to the ground motionless, with terrified eyes, defeat written across his face. Regaining his composure, Craig began scanning the room.

On the far side under glowing lights he noticed a set of machines filled with endless levers, dials and buttons; some flashing in sporadic bursts. A baffling maze of colourful connecting wires was visible. He paused with interest, wondering. Guided by his curiosity he made his way over. Running his fingers along the machines, he began manipulating the controls at random. Then from behind he heard a faint hum. Turning, a secret room opened before him, the walls pulling away from each other at the centre point. His eyes grew wide in awe, tinged with fascination.

Steadily, with eager steps, he disappeared inside, the floor hard and shiny. Displayed before him stood a huge glass sphere. Odd-looking machines lay around it, humming and discharging mechanical sounds. Inside the sphere vague shapes swam in a milky fire, moving back and forth as if they were alive, pulsing and glowing, diffusing an illumination from seemingly no source.

This must be the life sphere, he thought to himself, wiping cold nervous sweat from his forehead. He took a step back; again the wave of fascinated awe swept through him. Raising the gun with feverish anger, he fired, blowing it into a racket of shivering flames and sparks. The sound became deafening, the surrounding machines melting into liquid in the raging flames of fire with alarming speed. He closed his lips tightly, his eyes narrowly open. The air had become toxic, thick and heavy, clouded with a foul unearthly odour. It began choking and blinding him. His mind spun. Panic-stricken, he fought his way out and fled to the elevator.

In passing he noticed that the guard was now no longer there. An alarm suddenly activated, shrilling through the building, constant and unending. All the lights began to fade into complete darkness. Reaching ground level, he dashed out through the rear entrance into the rain. From the distance he could vaguely hear an ominous rumble of distorted voices. All he could think of now was Connie. He sprinted on through the thickening darkness, splashing into the drenched road, whitish-yellow candles of city light marking his way.

Within a matter of seconds he reached the hover-car, puffing and red-faced, barely recapturing his breath. Through the windscreen he saw Connie lying back against the seat, the dim moonlight reflecting against her. She appeared unmistakably motionless; not even a faint twitch. As he flipped the door open, he moved over with concerned alarm. He searched for a pulse; he could vaguely hear her heart thumping. Slowly, the beat began to weaken, drowned out by the sound of fusing circuit boards and failing mechanical components, a curl of smoke rising from her half-opened mouth. Her eyes were lifeless, wide open; set with an inorganic quality. With agonising surprise he realised she was an Android; another machine. He went to open his mouth, trying to bring forth words. It was no use - he was gripped with confused emotion. It was stained across his face; etched into his features.

Faint hope stirred him as he began a futile attempt to revive her, prodding at her, but for what? Then, from above, a hover-car descended, landing to the side of the road; a sleek black Air-Cruiser, aerodynamic, enveloped in a blanket of mist. A figure emerged. He was dressed in a long dark raincoat, wearing special black glasses used to magnify images like mini-binoculars. Correcting them, he stood there, calm and cool in the unending rain.

"Craig De Lucas?"

He stepped out from the car, tossing his gun onto the ground.

"Yes."

"Dick Marshall, Secret Agent - I guess you beat me to it…"

Craig stood without expression.

"Is the girl okay?"

He looked towards the drenched road. His face said it all with muted clarity.

"Another Android… Incredible. Some were so well-made, they didn't know themselves what they were…"

There was a brief pause; the rain intensified and a gush of wind swept by, scattered debris rustling softly across the city road.

"What now?" Craig muttered, his soaked hair covering his forehead, water drops running down creases on his drooping face.

"It's all over for you. Time to start afresh, rebuilding your life again."

The man began walking towards him, his cool facial expression fading into sympathetic concern. Reaching him, he halted, staring deeply into his dark eyes.

"Forget the woman, Craig. She wasn't real - just a machine… a highly advanced machine…"

Molecular Alteration

Jack's face sagged with age, his fragile body old and withered; the pale yellow moonlight shining in his eyes. His mind was now fixed, set by the agency which had convinced him that rejuvenation could be attained. The concept gripped him; the dream and yearning grew as he pictured himself youthful.

Bent and leaning, he walked alone through the foggy town centre, his shoes scraping against the cobbled road. The streets were dead and bare, the occasional surface vehicle passing leisurely along the narrow roads. Above him grey cold street lights lit the deserted town, shining feebly in the dense gloom. The small town was nothing more than an old village; a place held back in time by its remoteness. A few houses and apartment blocks lay scattered within its perimeter; a startling contrast from the neighbouring futuristic cities.

Opening the wooden gate, he made his way to the door of his old decrepit cottage. Enclosed in the front garden was a small fishpond reflecting the night stars. A cold wind lashed at him, dragging him around as if he were caught in a rushing ocean tide. In the background he could hear the sound of rustling leaves, as a line of trees swayed ferociously from side to side, whipping the foul-smelling mists into his face. The door creaked open... Standing there was his wife, her green cardigan bulging at the waist.

"Jack... Where have you been?"

He coughed and then stepped in, his face red from the chill, his lips numb. With an effort he pulled off his overcoat, latching it into the closet. He was oozing with a renewed confidence; it was set across his face, his old faded grey eyes lit up.

"Marylou, we need to speak. It's about that agency — yes, that agency; the only agency in the world licensed to make drastic human alterations of cosmological proportions."

She lowered her spectacles with one finger, and then spoke out earnestly.

"I hope you're bluffing, Jack. You just can't seem to leave it alone. You'll never change, always full of dreams...a childish illusion."

"No, Marylou, this is not a dream; nor an illusion."

Gently he placed his arm over her shoulder, limping into the dimly-lit sitting room, his legs worn out; his feet like two hot bricks. On a wooden table stood a side lamp glowing, diffusing a buttery yellow illumination. Above the vision set hung a picture of Jack, grinning and youthful;

something he was hoping to regain. Walking over to his comfy armchair he sat leaning back, loosening his shirt and removing his necktie.

The warm cosy atmosphere was perfect; the ideal place to unwind and reflect. He gazed around with distracted eyes, focusing on his library of books stacked untidily in the corner of the room.

"Well, Jack…? Speak up, then," Marylou said with a commanding tone, the harsh quality temporarily gone from her voice; her eyes full of stubborn dignity.

Quietly he sat, like an excited child, calculating his words carefully, withdrawn in her presence. Adjusting himself in a nervous twitch, he began to explain.

"Marylou, I've finally reached a decision. I'm going in for the rejuvenation process; it's booked. I was at the agency today in New York. Wednesday's the appointment."

She was silent, wide-eyed and open-mouthed. In her mind she'd tried desperately to come to terms with the inevitable. For months he had rattled on about the agency; about regaining his youth. It was all he'd ever wanted. After an extended pause Jack continued.

"Darling, you know how much this means to me. I've waited years impatiently, saved up enough credits for it… It's just a simple process altering the molecular arrangement of a human body back to any chosen age; even a reversible process, as long as you do it within a twenty-four hour period with, no additional fee attached - how can you lose…? Just imagine, I can relive my youth again; extend my life. Marylou, it's everyone's dream. Perhaps you should consider it too…? We could start saving now… You and I, beginning a whole new chapter in our lives… It's going to be special to be twenty again!"

After a moment of hesitation she replied sharply, an urgent rasp in her voice.

"Twenty…that's the age you were when you married me. I was a pretty nineteen-year old, and now I'm sixty-nine - an old woman - and you want to return to twenty. Jack, listen to yourself; it's pointless. Emotional immaturity, that's all it is; a senseless sub-rational craving. I would never consider being young again. We have worked so hard; why waste all those credits? We could even buy one of those new lush city apartments. The years may have flown by – yes, I've aged, but I still have desires… I would love to spend the remaining years in a beautiful place."

There was no reply; the glow in his eyes said it all with muted clarity. His mind was so deeply entrenched with the concept that her words faded from him like raindrops with no effect; his decision was final. Gently, she lifted herself from the rocking chair, her large frame wobbling as she moved towards him. She smiled, yet her eyes were unable to mask her true emotions. She was sad, bitterly sad. Fifty years of marriage had flashed by; a life smouldered in memories of both tears and joy. Reaching over, she caressed him, rubbing her hand across his withered face.

In the morning Jack awoke; the night had passed in a flash. The sky was dull; rain pouring, hammering against the bedroom window. Towards the corner of the room the vision set was playing with muted volume. With bleary eyes and without volition he pulled the sheet covers aside, stepping out of bed, swaying and rubbing his bloated face. The vid-phone rang. Clutching the receiver, he answered; his voice low and strained.

"Jack Webster..."

"Good morning, Sir. This is Doctor Ridley; I trust you're well."

"Yes Doctor," he replied, flushing a little.

"I'm calling to remind you that a company car is coming to pick you up tomorrow. It will drive you here directly. It's a Land-Cruiser; the latest and finest edition - of course, complementary."

"Thank you, Doctor. I had forgotten all about it. Oh, just one question... Tell me, is there a chance that I could get a lift back home after the process has been completed? I'm sorry, I don't mean to sound rude."

"Had you let me finish, you wouldn't have had to ask. It has all been taken care of."

"I don't know what to say... Thank you, doctor."

"Don't mention it, Sir. Well, I think I've covered all that I had to. The Land-Cruiser will arrive tomorrow at 9am sharp; till then, see to it that you get plenty of rest. Have a great day..."

The vid-phone went dead. He placed it down, mopping his forehead; clearing his vision. Walking to his cupboard, he reached for his cotton white hanky, drying nervous tears from his eyes. Inside he was torn with mixed emotions, although delighted he knew that his life was about to drastically change. Inching his way to the door, he slowly walked down the stairway, gripping the wooden banister for support. His legs grew weak; pausing, he took a breath and moved down a little further.

Entering the sitting room, he sat on his armchair, his thoughts and mind drifting and reflecting. Reaching over to the coffee table, he grabbed his smoking pipe and a small sack of deluxe tobacco, the finest brand. Shakily he lit up, and then sat back taking a long steady puff, creating a nimbus of grey smoke, bits of tobacco drifting to the rug. His eyes closed; he pictured himself youthful and strong, blurred images of his life rippling through his mind. For a time Jack drifted asleep; a sudden tug on his shoulder awoke him.

"Jack, wake up. You've been sleeping for hours; it's already past midday. I've fixed you some lunch…it's waiting in the kitchen."

There was a strong aroma of hot stew. As she exited the room, Jack scrambled to his feet, following behind her silk nightgown which was dragging across the floor.

"Marylou, wait! The agency called me this morning." He paused, regaining his breath. *"A Land-Cruiser is picking me up tomorrow at 9am…"*

She turned, sad eyes staring back at him; her mouth opened and closed but no sounds came. Limping over, Jack stood in front of her, his face still drowsy, a faint smirk twitching across his lips.

"You're really going to see this through, aren't you?" she said with a soft tone, almost inaudible.

"Marylou, we've already discussed this…"

"You just can't let go," the pitch in her voice rose. *"You're not even listening! Just be happy with what you are. Think about the consequences. What's going to become of you? Where's this journey going to lead to?*

"To my youth," he replied, *"To the agency Restoration Incorporated."*

Without reply she turned, heading for the kitchen and shaking her head; the oven hissing, filling the corridor with warm fumes. He yawned, stretching with a somewhat hypnotic, stubborn glare to his eyes.

As he walked into the sitting room he switched on the long screen vision set; there was a commercial. *"Old? Bored with your life? Want to experience being young again? Then call us, Restoration Incorporated… A guaranteed one-off journey back to your youth… A place where your dreams become a reality."* A number followed, and the commercial ended. He stood transfixed; his face said it all. *"I guess this is my destiny,"* he grumbled to himself. The word destiny was playing over and over in his mind.

As the day passed by, a new morning approached; against distant broken hills the sun rose. Then from the shrill of his alarm clock he awoke battering it into silence; his heart pulsating, the cords in his neck flexing with each beat.

"Damn… This alarm clock is always malfunctioning - it's 8.56."

Holding on to the side cabinet, he slipped out of bed, moving towards the closet. Inside hung his favourite grey suit, one which he used only for special occasions. For a moment he paused, scratching his head reflectively. Grabbing it, he sat on a bench removing his multi-coloured pyjamas with a straining effort. Behind, Marylou awoke; her plump face pallid and drooping. Rubbing her eyes, she then placed on her spectacles.

Instantly her vision came into focus. At that moment the doorbell rang; his heart skipped a beat.

"Quick, go answer. It's probably the chauffer – hurry!"

As she left the room, heading for the front door, he rose to his feet, splashing on some cologne across his coarse face; it left a sharp and bitter scent. Hurriedly, he limped out, creeping down the stairway a step at a time. Reaching the foyer, he glanced at the mirror, his reflection staring back at him. Pulling out a comb, he brushed back a few strands of wispy grey hair. Behind him Marylou stood watching, her face contorted with an expression of displeasure and concern.

"Marylou, this is a new start for me…a new beginning."

"Yes indeed, Jack, a new beginning for you… But what about us? I don't want to be young again…"

"When I'm back we'll talk. Trust me, it will all work out."

Leaving the house, he hugged her affectionately, the clicking sound of his heels diminishing as he headed towards the metallic-silver Land-Cruiser. The chauffer came out opening the back door; he manufactured a grin and made it shine across his face, his teeth sparkling white. Jack looked at him apologetically for his brief delay.

"Good morning, Sir. Please make yourself comfortable. We should reach New York City by 10.30. At the back you have a small vision set, a radio and a mini-bar with some refreshments."

Jack chuckled in vacant amusement. He appeared calm and content, yet deep down there was a feeling of apprehension growing inside him. As the time was drawing nearer he began to feel anxious; he was caught inwardly, gripped with conflicting emotions. Entering, he turned towards Marylou who stood at the doorway, fixed to the spot. She waved repeatedly, flicking her spectacles towards her face, repressing the impulse to cry.

Well over an hour had passed; ahead stood the city. Switching through the various channels on the vision set, Jack snapped off the power. He laid back, his eyelids heavy and drooping. He grew restless and impatient. Even the constant flow of conditioned air was becoming an annoyance to him.

"Excuse me, chauffeur… How long to go?"

"Quarter of an hour and we'll be there, Sir."

A tingling sensation swept through him from head to toe. Peering from the window, he caught a brief glimpse of the city. Passing under a short road tunnel the scene periodically vanished, reappearing moments later. He cleared his eyes, looking again; it momentarily deflected his attention. The entire city was erupting into life; a torrent of excited human activity, endless streams of people, air cars and glider-cycles - such a distinct contrast from the tiny insignificant village he had come from. His deep sunken eyes widened with excitement, his heart leaping; in a short while he would be part of it all.

The chauffeur sat silently, glancing at Jack's reflected image in the mirror. He studied him for a time.

"So, Sir, you're going in for the rejuvenation process, right?"

"Yes, that's right," he said excitedly.

"My Dad was thinking about it; however, he suddenly changed his mind."

Jack's ears perked up.

"He told me that life has its seasons, and that you can never recapture those moments in time, no matter what. Going back would be meaningless... Nothing at the end can stand the test of time..."

Jack paused, absorbing the somewhat philosophical words; he raised his finger to his mouth in thought. The Land-Cruiser turned sharply into a narrow side street; driving a little further, it slid to a smooth halt at the curb before a shimmering skyscraper.

"Here you go, Sir - we're here."

Without reply Jack looked out, staring at the huge glass structure, his eyes squinting into focus.

"Excuse me, do you have a phone? I'd like to call my wife."

"Sure, no problem," the chauffeur replied with unusual eloquence.

Pressing a button, a coloured phone slid out in front of Jack from a concealed compartment. He lifted the receiver and began dialling. Then he decided to end the call. He knew Marylou was distressed; there were no words of comfort, nothing other than a change of heart from his side would do. Grabbing the handle, he opened the door. Hurriedly, the chauffeur rushed out.

"Allow me, Sir..."

Jack stepped out, holding onto the chauffeur for support. A rush of blood to the head made him momentarily dizzy; his mind spun.

"Thank you, young man."

"Don't mention it, Sir; it's my job."

From his pocket, Jack pulled out a few loose credits. After briefly calculating the amount, he handed them over with a warm, piercing smile.

"Here you go..."

The chauffeur grinned.

"Thank you; really, there was no need… Can I assist you any further?"

"No, I'll be fine," he replied with a self-satisfied calmness.

Shaking his hand, Jack turned around, walking towards the attractively inviting doorway. There he halted and with attention read the shifting coloured neon sign: 'RESTORATION INCORPORATED'. He began to wonder… *Is this really going to fulfil me…fill that gap in my life which I so desperately long for?* *This is certainly the closest thing to immortality; man's greatest quest and desire since the very beginning of time.* Pressing the buzzer, a young lady instantly approached. Pulling the glass doors open, she smiled.

"Welcome, Mr Webster. We've been anticipating your arrival. Please come this way."

Jack was captivated by her beauty and soft feminine voice. It had an unusual quality about it, one which inspired calmness and total assurance. She was a tall young lady with full red lips; the whites of her eyes sparkled, her hair long and curly, her tight blue dress fitting perfectly around her sculptured figure and slender shoulders.

Taking in a breath of air, he walked through the dazzling polychromatic shimmer of the doorway into the building. In the reception area was a group of elderly people lying back on a comfy white sofa; in their hands they were filling out forms. A couple of suited gentlemen stood around, explaining and pointing. The stone patterned walls glittered; a large analogue clock hung pleasantly. Entering the elevator, they headed to the ninth floor. The young lady stood close by cheerfully.

"Nervous?"

"A touch," he muttered with surprising speed as he gazed at her in stunned admiration.

"Don't be. We have people calling all the time booking in with us; list after list of letters coming in with monotonous regularity - we've got a busy schedule here."

As the elevator doors slid open, he walked out, finding himself in a large reception area, recorded music playing softly in the background. The air was filled with a floral perfume, sweet and enchanting. He paused, taking in the scene, his reflection scattered across the mirrored ceiling, the soft notes of music easing his now fatigued mind.

Picking up a receiver, the receptionist said into it, *"Mr Webster has arrived, Doctor."* Her modest eyes deflected away, focusing on Jack. *"He won't be a moment, Sir."*

After a brief but frustrating delay, Dr Ridley came walking over; a middle-aged, genial looking man with a head full of neatly arranged hair.

"*Great to see you again, Mr Webster. I trust your journey was pleasant. Please come this way.*"

He smiled encouragingly, his eyes a deep blue; strong, wide and inviting. Jack took an unsteady breath and advanced without reply. The hour he'd so longed for had finally arrived; there was now no turning back - at least, that's how he felt. What happened next solely depended on the Doctor, he thought to himself bravely. Walking along, the receptionist turned, smiling his way. He blushed, his attention briefly deflected. After a slow walk down the hallway they reached a white door: Room E. With the faint motion of the doctor's hand before the code beam, the door opened before them. Stepping in, he sat on his swivel chair, pulling himself towards his desk. A handful of documents lay neatly piled on top, a gold-plated fountain pen resting to the side. Everything in the room was spotless, arranged with mathematical precision; the sign of a high profile agency.

"*Mr Webster, please take a seat,*" he said, waving his slender hand.

Inching over, he sat on a comfy white chair, a mixture of emotions and sensations twisting through him. Pulling out a file from inside the drawer, the doctor leafed through the sheets of paper, his eyes moving as he absorbed the information. Then the intercom speaker on his desk buzzed, the small image of the receptionist forming on the screen. "*Doctor Ridley, Mr Quinn just called. He's postponed his appointment again. He's now available on Tuesday.*"

"*That's fine, Deb, book him in as usual.*"

The image on the screen dimmed and vanished. Looking towards Jack, he smiled with a suave confidence, his face set with reflected glory.

"*Right, first things first. I see from your initial application you wanted to return back to the age of twenty; that is correct, is it not?*"

Clasping and wringing his hands, he replied, "*Yes, it is.*"

"*Well now, before we can commence any further I need you to sign the contract. It includes all the legalities and clauses. However, before that, I need to make certain that you are fully aware of one absolute fact.*"

He paused. Jack leaned forward eagerly and with his eyes urged him on.

"*After the transformation, if you decide to revert back to your current age, it will have to be within the first twenty-four hours. After that the process will be totally irreversible; your body will be set for life at a molecular level. There will be no going back. I hope I've made myself perfectly clear. To even attempt to go back would be fatal*" *for any organic life system. Also, as I'm sure you are aware, the process can only work once - it's a one-time change."*

"Yes, doctor, I'm aware of the facts. I've read all the leaflets and information manuals you've supplied me with, not to mention your many letters."

"Good...so I presume you are happy to commence with the process...?"

Without reply, he nodded in agreement, yet the glow in his eyes suggested that he was tussling with his emotions, a natural biological response to such a life-altering decision.

"Now...as to the small matter of the payment...I assume you want to pay off the remaining balance today?"

"Oh, of course," Jack mumbled with a slight look of embarrassment. From his pocket he yanked out 5000 credits, waving it into the doctor's face.

"Oh doctor - just one question."

"Go ahead," he replied with a keen elaborated casualness.

"Tell me, will my memory be affected in anyway? Will I still have a clear recollection of all of my life...all my seventy years?"

"Your memory will not be affected or altered in anyway. If anything, it will be clearer and sharper than you could have ever imagined. Here, check this out."

From the desk he pressed a button. Snapping his fingers, he pointed into the corner of the room; a hologram began to form, glowing into existence. A young woman stood, giving a brief account of her transformation. Minutes later the image faded, the oscillating haze with it.

"Any more questions?" he raised his hands with a big slanting smile; it had no veiled overtones.

"None..." Jack's voice broke off suddenly with a ripple of excitement.

"As soon as you sign the document, we can commence. You can be totally guaranteed that it is painless; as painless as sitting on a beach topping up your tan. It's a known statistic: one hundred percent."

Holding the fountain pen, Jack's hand began to shiver. Inside he was torn with mixed emotions, yet the burning desire to regain his youth was too much for him to contain. He was compelled to see it through. Pulling the document towards him, he signed. As he placed the pen down the lights began to fade, the doctor staring at him in the half-light. From an opening in the wall, a long tube-like bed retracted out a highly sophisticated piece of machinery with an elaborate design. As the tube opened up it diffused a pale illumination that spread over everything, almost ghostly. Gradually it began to radiate heat; a warm, mild heat. The wall behind now appeared to fade in the glowing light, turning almost transparent. He sat still, with awe and reverence.

"Sir, it's time…"

"I hope nothing goes wrong," Jack said, swallowing nervously, his face showing doubt.

"Don't allow your thalamic impulses to take control; you've nothing to fear."

Jack rose from the chair holding the doctor's hand. This seemingly simple process was about to defy the laws of both science and time, like a tidal wave moving back through the ages. Walking over, he began to feel calm and secure, his doubts and fears slowly subsiding. He paused watching the pale light oozing out with brilliance, yet with no effect on his eyes. Drawing closer, he became captivated by the light. He felt the heat enveloping him, warming him inwardly. Leaning over, he lay still, resting on the machine. Instantly the tube began to close, locking into place. Jack was now immersed in the heat and glowing light, warming his wrinkled body. From the machine a computer slid out, a wide screen, complex-looking. The doctor then began inputting various bits of data; name, address - standard information. His lean body was bent like a coiled spring, his warm eyes focused and set, his conceptual faculties operating with maximum attention. *"Commence scanning process,"* he instructed the computer. The vocal signal activated it into operation; the screen sparked into life and began the monitoring assessment of Jack's genetic make-up. It presented him with various readings, such as body temperature, blood pressure and body mass. It then displayed a series of brain wave patterns; stress and fear levels appeared normal. Pressing a large red button, it all began…

Suddenly Jack was showered in sparks, sparks which penetrated his skin. At that moment his bodily composition began to alter; his thin old frame filling out, his muscles and flesh stretching, replenished with life and energy. Across his face, grey wrinkles and lines began dimming away, his skin tightening, soft and youthful. His dark sunken eyes were now fleshy; his wispy strands of hair had thickened, enriched with colour, texture and moisture. A whole array of alterations now began to take place to the point in time of his request.

After a few minutes the machine stopped; the light and heat fading with it. The process had been completed, his entire body rejuvenated at an astounding rate.

He lay there breathing slowly, his eyes closed tightly with expectancy. His heart was beating with vigour, gradual comprehension coming to him.

Slowly the machine began to open, the doctor standing over, looking towards him. Jack was motionless, recapturing a moment in time that had passed many years before.

"Mr Webster, how are you feeling? You look fantastic."

As he opened his eyes he became fully conscious. With a sudden unexpected leap of delight, Jack rose to his feet with alarming ease. Rushing to a long mirror, he stood in amazement, his mouth hanging in disbelief. He touched his face, running his hand through his thick dark hair, his eyes sparkling full of life and vitality.

"Look... Look at me doctor, it's incredible."

His voice rose with energy; it was alive - deep with quality, clear and sharp. The transformation was spot-on. He was now back; back to the age of twenty, just as he had requested. The door swung open and two male technicians walked in; their piercing acknowledgement of his presence was clear to see. There was a faint ripple of applause.

"Mr Webster, you look great..."

The doctor quickly butted in suavely.

"Mr Webster, the technicians are here to take a few measurements. The agency always supplies our clients with a new suit to wear after the transformation. It's for you to keep as a memento."

After a short interval they had taken the appropriate measurements, and within minutes Jack was changing into a dapper cream-coloured suit with matching trousers and a pair of finely polished black shoes. Walking over to the doctor, he smiled.

"Doc, I can't find words to express my emotions. This is all I have ever dreamt of; a dream that has now become a reality."

Taking a business card, they shook hands; he was now on his way. As Jack left the building, noonday sunlight streamed down on him, a mild breeze encircling the air. Formless clouds began to sweep away, leaving the skyline bright and cheerful. He paused, scratching the tip of his nose, his mind reflecting and drifting in his own delight. A horn sounded loudly. He looked up. Parked to the side of the road was the silver Land-Cruiser. The window lowered.

"Hi, Mr Webster..."

Jack briskly made his way over. Swinging the door open, he sat inside, his eyes glazed with delight. He could see his reflection scattered across the window; he liked what he saw. Not even the few words that came from the chauffeur were able to deflect him from his somewhat hypnotic state of ecstasy; he was wallowing in it. After a seemingly short drive, Jack was almost home; he was lying still, half dozing. Then the Land-Cruiser stopped, parking outside the small cottage.

"Sir, we've arrived."

Lifting his head from the cushioned seat, he looked over. An odd sensation swept over him. He wondered why, but had no answers. Pulling out a handful of credits from his trouser pocket, he placed them into the chauffeur's hand.

As the Land-Cruiser drove away, disappearing into the distance, Jack rushed over towards the cottage. He had a sharp feeling, a lingering intuition that something was wrong. The surroundings were oddly different; even the air had its own unusual scent to it. Halting for a time, he noticed that the street was now darker in the shade of great towering trees. Walking forward, he went to push open the wooden gate, but it wasn't there. His brows rose in bewilderment. Slowly, he advanced towards the door, his eyes shifting like a speeding pendulum moving in rhythmic analytic motion. Even the fishpond had gone, now covered with long grass and decaying weeds; all the flowers around had been trampled flat, some torn loose from the soil.

He chuckled to himself in disbelief and then shrugged his shoulders philosophically. Beyond the lace curtains of the cottage window, dim shapes were visible, stirring around. Before he could reach the door it opened. Standing there was an old man, his chest rising and falling with the effort of breathing, a sharp stench of tobacco seeping from his breath. His face was hard and lined, unshaven; his light green eyes fading in with his pallid, wrinkling complexion.

"Yes, can I help you?" he said flatly.

Jack froze on the spot. Reassuming a measure of composure, he lifted his finger and then hesitantly replied.

"Do I know you?"

The old man paused momentarily, his face twisting in ironic amusement.

"I'm sorry, I should be asking you that; you're the one knocking at my house."

Jack was lost for words, overwhelmed with the stark realisation of his peculiar predicament. He stepped back, glancing around avidly as if he were examining the area, his pulse racing in and out of rhythm.

Perhaps he'd made a mistake? *But no, it couldn't be,* he thought to himself, *I know my own house.* Moving to the door, he angrily spoke out.

"Quit fooling me around, old man. Where's Marylou?"

Rapidly, the old man raised his hand. He opened his mouth as if to shout but then refrained, slamming the door shut. Jack was enraged; the anger was clear to see as his face became hard. Racing over, he pressed the buzzer, banging his fists.

"Open up...!"

After a wild attempt to break the door down he halted, gradual comprehension coming to him. He took a step back and composed himself. At that moment the door opened. A young woman approached, the old man concealing himself behind the stairway. Jack stood staring at this woman he had never seen before.

"I'm very sorry... There must be some kind of misunderstanding."

Jack looked on without uttering a word.

"Are you sure you're at the right house? There's no one called Marylou here. We've lived here for the last five years... We purchased the property back in August 1965. No one to my knowledge has lived here prior to us by that name."

"1965!" His voice rose. *"I thought you said you've been living here five years?"*

"Yes, that's right."

"But how...? How is this possible?"

The hackles of his neck rose, his voice breaking off suddenly. He stuttered into a torment of incomprehension. The woman stood quietly without reply.

"Tell me, what date is it?"

"Why it's the 21st of August........."

"But what year?"

She hesitated, constraining the emotion to laugh; for a moment it almost overcame her. She was left in dumbfounded amazement.

"It's 1970... August 1970."

Jack felt himself go inwardly still, the colour from his face draining a sickly white. He paused, unable to mutter a word. His faculties appeared to have abandoned him temporarily. The whole scene had become an episode from a bad dream, only this time there was no waking up. *"This wasn't part of the package,"* he mumbled to himself. *"Perhaps I'm experiencing some kind of psychotic interlude, a self-induced hallucination."*

As the faint blur disappeared from him, he began to condense his thoughts into a semblance of rationality. It was now clear what was transpiring; not only had he returned to the tender age of twenty, but he was now also living within that reality... 1970. Staring at him, the woman began to feel compassionate, fearing he'd lost his mind.

"Is there anything I can do for you...? Perhaps a taxi...or a ride into town?"

Jack turned away speechless, walking towards the road, his feet sweeping loosely against the granite pathway, a look of dejection across his face. Behind, the lady stood watching, shutting the door moments later. Cycling towards him was the paper boy, his cheeks red and dimpled, his white cap turned sideways across his head. As he sped by, he threw a newspaper onto the road. Kneeling down, Jack picked it up in a somewhat weary motion. At the top, printed in black ink, was the date '21 August 1970.'

Racing through the roads, he soon discovered that the entire village had changed. Houses he remembered well were no longer there; ones that were seemed dramatically altered from the way he remembered them. A burst of cold sweat broke out across his face. He paused, regaining his breath, resting his hands on his hips. Lifting his head he heard voices in the distance. The village was alive with growing sound; people walking by, going about their day. Silently, he walked on with growing interest; a row of familiar shops lay ahead. Across the street he heard the sound of jazz music playing from a bar. He stopped and then began to walk over, guided by his curiosity.

Parting the flap doors, he stepped in, his thoughts and mind wandering with the sounds of jazz and clinking beer bottles. Ripples of laughter and murmurs drifted to him noisily, voices rising wildly. A dense layer of cigarette smoke lingered in the air, creating a faint haze around the bar. To the corner lay a pool table, balls scattered across it, the cue stick lying on top. Then, at that moment, he recalled that the bar was one he had come to during his teenage years; yet it wasn't quite the same. Gazing around, he noticed a familiar face - familiar in a blurred, distorted fashion which he could not pinpoint... Then he remembered brightly, it was Bruce the bartender. He studied him closely; his burly frame, his broad face and lined forehead. Unexpectedly Bruce signalled over to him, waving his hand.

"Hey Jack! Come over."

Jack remained still, a glare of astonishment oozing from his eyes as he gazed through the sea of faces before him. Regaining his composure, he pushed his way through a crowd up to the bar.

"Hey, what's up? Is everything okay? Looks like you've just seen a ghost," Bruce blasted in comical concern. Pouring him a glass of whisky, he placed it in front of him.

"Here, it's on the house."

Jack loosened his collar, wiping his forehead with his sleeve. He then gripped the glass, gulping down the shot of chilled whisky in jerky agitation.

"Feeling better?"

"I'm not too sure," Jack replied with a noticeable hint of growing confusion building in his clipped voice.

"Bruce... Can I ask you something?"

"Yes, what is it?"

Jack licked his lips pensively.

"It is August 1970, isn't it?"

Bruce stared vacantly, his face contorted in mystification. A strange cold smile played about his lips.

"Yes, that's right... Jack, are you sure you're okay?"

Without reply he nodded absently, then reached out his hand, placing it on Bruce's shoulder, almost yanking him off balance.

"Fix me a double..."

Reaching for a clean glass, he poured more whisky, placing it into Jack's hand. A restless stir moved through the bar. There were murmurs and coughs, as a queue of customers waited impatiently to be served.

"Listen, I've got to start serving... Go take a seat - we'll chat later."

As Jack turned away, Marylou walked in. He gasped, his hand flying up to his mouth, cold shock knotting his stomach. She stood there; young, her long blonde hair wavy and groomed, her face slender and chiselled, just as he recalled. By her side was a young man, dressed in a black leather jacket, blue jeans, hair slicked back and greased, a piece of gum fixed between his teeth. Jack watched on, his jaw hanging from his face in disbelief.

Gripping the glass of whisky tightly, he knocked it back greedily, leaving his breath reeking with the stench of alcohol. His mind spun. Shakily he reached over to the bar, placing the empty glass down. He was slowing feeling the effects of the drink. Composing himself, he staggered over towards Marylou. His legs felt weightless, his face inexpressive and unyielding. Then, bringing his eyes into sharp focus, he studied her every move; her smile, the motion of her moving lips.

Within a matter of seconds he had reached the table. Pulling out a chair, he sat, running his fingers nervously against his leg. His expression became fixed rigidly in place. The young man then turned to him, losing his gum, sticking it to a glass ashtray. His eyes widened swiftly.

"Hey, you're Jack Webster! I'm Kieran, Dan's younger brother. Perhaps you don't recall...We met once...at the baseball ground."

At that very instant Jack searched his mind, thinking back through the years. Then he brightly recalled that Dan was an old school friend. He stuttered and coughed, a whole maze of thoughts and images hurdling through his mind; he tried to manufacture a smile but his face failed to respond.

"Hey buddy, are you okay? By the way, this is Marylou; Dan's wife."

Jack's face drained of colour and filled with panic as Marylou reached out her hand and smiled brightly. With lightning speed he leapt up and ran towards the exit, barging past a group of drunkards. As he dashed towards the end of the road, two youths turned, pointing and staring. Not only was he living in the past, but everything around had altered with it. Nothing was the same; a whole new chapter was unfolding before his very eyes. Slowing down, he leaned against a lamppost, puffing and red-faced. Gazing towards a row of houses, he saw bright lights seeping through curtained windows. He began to reminisce; a picture forming in his mind of a hot meal, his wife sitting close by drinking tea, a bright living room. These images began torturing him; he desperately wanted to be back. A strong wind blew around him, almost dragging him off-balance. The sky began to grow dark; nightfall was approaching, the pale moon appearing dimly in the half-light. Great silent evergreens rose dark and unmoving in the evening twilight. He gazed around in despair and defeat. Then, from seemingly nowhere, a cab driver stopped to the side of the road; the window lowered, his face bland and eager.

"Evening," he tipped his cap. *"Where to, buddy?"*

Sliding his hand into his breast pocket, Jack pulled out a handful of credits. He counted fretfully, the palms of his hands warm and sticky. Moving over, he leaned into the car, flicking the credits towards the driver's face, his voice high-pitched and rippling with nervous tension.

"This is all I've got... Please, I need to get to New York City."

Fiddling in his trouser pocket, he pulled out the business card for R.Incorp.

"Here, this is the address..."

His voice came out sharply in the cold air.

"I'm sorry, buddy... I know the city like the back of my hand; there's no such address."

Speedily, the cab drove away, leaving the smell of burning rubber in its trail. He looked up towards space; the endless sky and the hanging sphere of the moon his only comfort. At the corner of the road was a park. Hurriedly he walked over, resting under a tree, holding onto the grass and roots jutting out from the soil, his feet sinking into the lush foliage. Above his head a few gnats began circling around him. Outlined against the darkness of space, stars appeared; clusters of them twitching and flickering. He opened his eyes, gazing at the village; it evoked past memories now vivid in his mind, his face clouded in a haze of self-pity. A small tear trickled down his cheek, the cords in his neck flexing with the beating sound of his heart.

At that moment a car horn sounded, echoing through the cold night. It had a distinctive note to it, one which was familiar to him.

Jack caught his breath. Scrambling to his feet, he looked over. There in front of him was the Land-Cruiser, its sharp silver-metallic frame shining out under the streetlights. His eyes bulged in amazement, the edges of his mouth hanging in wonder. In a daze he began walking over, eager and apprehensive. Then the chauffer stepped out from the Cruiser, his face warm and soft.

"Are you ready, Mr Webster?"

As Jack advanced, his lips were unable to move, silenced by the astounding sequence of events. Calmly, he opened the door and then sat, the cold leather seats penetrating through his trousers and chilling him; a stretch of hairs rose from his arms like frozen spikes. Passing through the village, they drove over a bleak line of hills covered in a light mist. Jack was motionless, peering into the stillness of the night, the only sound coming from the echoes of his mind; echoes of confusion, fear, a whole concoction of elaborated emotions whizzing through him. He laid his head back wearily. To the left ran a winding road, disappearing into the mist. The mist didn't seem to pass, concealing the surrounding landscape. Jack closed his eyes, uncertain of what lay ahead. He felt a wave of dizziness and exhaustion; next, rolling clouds of blackness.

"Mr Webster… We've arrived."

He leapt up. To his astonishment, it was now morning. The sun was suspended in the distance, beaming down and warming the city. It all happened in a flash; it just didn't seem to connect with the ordinary flow of time. A whole scene of early morning activity was displayed before him. People were roaming the streets in their thousands, chatting and discussing, moving around feverishly.

Moving out of the Cruiser, Jack stood rigidly, his feet planted against the pavement. He blinked, adjusting to the light; his eyes were glazed like two sightless light-reflecting orbs. A cool breeze of air swirled around him. He straightened; in front stood the towering skyscraper, the glass doors wide apart, the same shifting colour neon sign, RESTORATION INCORPORATED.

On the floor lay a crumpled newspaper. Kneeling down, he read the date: March 2020. He now realised he was back; his heart thumped with the realisation, flooding his body with hope and confusion.

Lifting himself, he approached the building with eager steps. Walking in, he saw it was lifeless. He gazed around with a profound curiosity, passing his hand nervously through his hair. Everything was in place; the stone patterned walls, the hanging clock, but oddly, no one was in sight. Suddenly he turned. Striding towards him was Dr Ridley, that familiar smile widening across his face.

"It's surprising to see you so soon, Mr Webster…"

In a flurry of anger, Jack gripped him by the collar, a sorrowful light in his grey, pain-drenched eyes, his voice clipped and intense.

"What did you do to me…?"

The doctor jerked loose, staring eye to eye with him; yet he appeared calm and composed.

"Mr Webster, is something wrong?"

"You're damn right something's wrong. You cheated me." Sweat broke out across his face.

"No one cheated you, Mr Webster; no one. Perhaps you cheated yourself?"

Jack paused significantly, his resolve melting like wax. Something in the doctor's keen glance and voice bored into him, penetrating his depths. He waited for a time, as if contemplating a reply or waiting alertly for instruction. He was overwhelmed with confusion, mystified by the sequence of events, his anger fading as he began composing himself. Abruptly he spoke out, yet somewhat subdued, his face dry and bright with emotion.

"Send me back…back to what I was…"

Without reply, the doctor lifted his hand, directing him towards the elevators. His face had a peculiar glow about it. Within minutes they had reached the ninth floor. As the doors slid open, Jack approached the now familiar reception area.

"Please take a seat, Mr Webster. I won't keep you," the doctor said, walking away.

Without reply Jack sank into a chair, gazing at himself in the mirrored ceiling, clasping his hands; the minutes passing and his mind reeling. A sudden tap on his shoulder unnerved him. He turned. A blonde receptionist stood before him; one he hadn't seen before.

"Mr Webster, the doctor is now ready for you. It's Room E; down the hallway to your right..."

Picking himself up from the chair, he made his way. As he entered the room the tube-like bed was opened, glowing with the same heat and energy as before. In the half-light Jack's face was vaguely distinguishable. Lamely, he approached the machine, the doctor moving with him. Rubbing his head reflectively, Jack turned, facing the now smiling doctor.

"I just don't understand what happened... There is no rational explanation; somehow I went back in time. I was living in 1970...but not the 1970 I recalled..."

The doctor reached over to him, his face warm and expressive.

"Jack... A man's burning desire can create a virtual world that seems real to him, built from an overwhelming passion to recapture moments in time which have long passed. Returning back to the age of twenty was your wish, but in your mind and heart your true desire was to relive moments which have now ceased."

"But Doctor... If my experience was nothing but a subconscious construct of my mind wanting to relive my past, why were things different and not the way I recalled them?"

"Life passes us by very quickly, Jack. We spend our days toiling, worrying about our daily needs and worldly desires, but we seldom sit back and ask ourselves why... Why am I here? Where am I going? I'm a living miracle built up of atoms, molecules; a factory of living cells dwelling in a highly complex world teeming with wonders and life, floating in the depths of Space... A universe without limit or end... You are special, Jack. It would be pointless to go back in time...and even if it were plausible...things could never be the same, not even in your dreams, not even in the deepest depths of your mind. It's your future that matters; not your past. The one question I leave you with is 'where'... Where is your life journey taking you, Jack...?"

Jack was silent. These deep words had triggered off an inner chain reaction. It made him reflect. Indeed, it was the first time in his life that he had heard words of such profundity and meaning. The doctor smiled a smile of complete assurance and tenderness.

Lying on the machine, the process commenced. His bright sparkling eyes began to fade, his tight soft skin loosening and crinkling, his colour-filled face draining pale and old. Within a matter of seconds his body shuddered, altering strangely, shifting back into an elderly withered man with molecular precision, all his worldly desires eradicated with it.

Leaving the building, the silver Land-Cruiser pulled out, stopping in front. Jack's vision was now hazed, slightly out of focus; blinding relief flooding over him. The sky was spilling over with a glowing radiance, one which stretched high up into the atmosphere. Air-cars now became distinguishable as they hovered above; others darted into the horizon. He gazed towards the blue, smiling. All he wanted now was to hold Marylou in his arms. Edging over to the Cruiser, the window lowered, and a husky voice sounded.

"Mr Webster, are you ready?"

An expression of serenity manifested itself across his face from cheek to cheek, his old fragile frame quivering in the blowing wind. Inside he sank into the soft seats, his arms folding neatly across his lap. Resting his head back, the Cruiser began moving away.

The drive home was brisk; he was almost there. Entering the village, they passed a narrow stream with slanting moss-covered banks; large trees swaying modestly in the breeze, their supple trunks moist with spring sap. Jack lowered the window, staring out towards a distant line of green hills, some lost in the dazzling morning light. A flock of birds glided silently above; he could smell the sweet scent of candy floss and frying popcorn. A colourful cluster of helium-filled balloons swept the air, covering the sky; a group of youths roamed the streets playfully. It was a carnival atmosphere; a cheering start to the day. As the Land-Cruiser stopped by the cottage, the chauffeur moved out, plucking the door open.

"After you, Sir."

Slowly Jack stepped out onto the road, dazed and weak, his heart labouring, yet a spark of joy oozed from within him. He sighed contently. Stretching his arms, he inhaled. The air was good; filled with the scent of growing plants. Earth was thriving with vitality, plants and foliage growing harmoniously in all directions; bugs and insects, everything in symbiosis... *What was it that set life into motion?* he suddenly thought to himself as he became ever so receptive to the things he once held as insignificant. Walking towards the cottage, the paper boy came peddling over on his bicycle, his red dimpled cheeks wobbling, his green baseball cap turned sideways across his head.

"Morning, Mr Webster..."

As he sped by he flung a newspaper onto the lawn, smiling cheerfully, disappearing into the distance. Opening the gate, Jack walked on towards the door crookedly. To the side he saw the fishpond, a small green toad hopping from leaf to leaf. Crawling on the ground was an army of ants going through the mysterious intricate process of building, and carrying tiny pieces of debris back to their base. Jack stood back, fascinated by these miniature organic life forms labouring; it made him reflect in wonder at just how precious and amazing life was. Although his days were passing, draining away before him, something more beautiful lay ahead. Within the spectrum of the universe he knew that his life had meaning and significance; that death wasn't the end but a possible new beginning. Taking a breath of air, he walked on unhindered. Before he could ring the buzzer, the door opened. Standing there was Marylou, enthralled with joy, ripples of emotion twisting through her. He embraced her tightly, kissing her again and again, his lips warm against her cheek. The long, tiresome journey was now over...

Mechanical Eyes

The year was 3010. R.M SPECIAL TECHNOLOGIES had built the first city in outer space. They had made remarkable advancements in the field of Biomechanics. Robotic Evolution had reached soaring heights. For the brilliant minds who helped carve a new chapter in Science, something more sinister lay ahead...

Tossing the bed sheets aside, I flicked on the light switch. My heart was pounding, frigid perspiration rising to the surface of my skin. As usual, I'd had the same recurring nightmare; one with which I had become all too familiar. My only comfort came from the knowledge that my wife Jane lay there beside me.

"Michael, are you okay? That dream, I bet...?"

"Yeah... Just the same one, night after night..."

"Sweetheart, I think it's about time you take a break from work. Maybe we should go on a space cruise, a few weeks out on Mars... the perfect place for you to unwind. We could even book into one of those health resorts... Just think; you and me together, trudging through the valleys and gazing at the sun from an alien world."

"Yeah, maybe you're right...but I don't know if that's the answer. I'd best get some sleep."

Switching off the lights, I lay still in a cold sweat. The tiled floor reflected the glow of the moonlight, the howling wind sweeping insistently against the bedroom window.

In the morning the sound of my alarm chronometer awoke me, the overhead vision screen activating with a news flash: *'Good morning, Chicago! Robot child-carers now available for hire at your nearest supermarket.'* I sat up, switching the sharp-voiced alarm clock into nullification. Through the blinds I saw the sun shimmering softly, a ball of energy gloating in the air.

Bleary-eyed, I struggled out of bed and prepared for work; changing into my pinstripe suit, dabbing a splash of cologne across my cheeks. A cold, clipped formality. From the door the mini-robot whizzed over to me holding a tray of tea and biscuits, its soft metallic voice sounding, the notes of classical music drifting in the background.

"Good morning, Michael... Would you like some breakfast?"

Soundlessly I deactivated it, leaving it still; I was in no mood to dialogue. From the rotating mirror I caught a glimpse of Jane's reflection as she lay there dead asleep, a beam of yellow sunlight resting over her naked body.

As I exited the house I walked towards the car. With the snapping command of my fingers the door flipped open, the steering wheel slid out from its concealed safety compartment. A faint breeze encircled the surrounding air. The morning sky was bright, a contrasting reflection of my emotions.

Activating the autopilot, I was now on my way, still deeply troubled by the ongoing nightmares. Knowing I had a busy day ahead, I tried to flush it out of my mind; it was imperative. Working as a robotic engineer required the ultimate attention, especially with R.M Special Technologies, the most advanced engineering company in the world. They were responsible for building cities in outer space, along with the finest robotic machinery to help in the colonisation of other planets; antigravity technology had revolutionised space travel as well as life on Earth.

A short distance away stood the entrance, the same familiar flashing sign: 'Welcome to R.M. Special Technologies.' It was a huge complex buzzing with activity. Thrusting the lever, the car accelerated, gaining rapid momentum; a short burst of speed was all it needed. Within seconds I had arrived. Outside, patrolling the site was a team of police troopers; organic robots, advanced humanoids - unusual for this time of day. Turning to me, they saluted. Passing my hand over the code beam, the security bars lifted. I drove through.

I was now in my office, lying back on the chair, gazing at a series of satellite images of Europa. It had been newly colonised; no longer a deserted ball of frozen liquid and hydrothermal vents, it was now a planet littered with metal structures, teeming with human life. To explore its ocean was the next major project in the hope of finding alien marine life. Drilling into the Europan ice crust was going to be a major challenge. Spinning a dial, the hologram faded with immediate effect. Then, unexpectedly, there was a knock at the door. Doug walked in tossing his jacket over his shoulder.

"Hey Michael, you made it on time today."

"Just about."

"What's up? You don't look yourself."

"Doug... Have you ever had a nightmare before...? I mean, the same one night after night?"

Raising both hands, he gestured in dismissal.

"I'd be lying to say I had. It's probably just stress; don't worry about it. Besides, you've got so much work to do; that means you'll have no time to worry about some silly dream of yours, okay? If you need me, you know where I am. Catch you later – oh, and give my regards to Jane."

For an extended period I sat immobile and silent, looking through a pile of documents that lay scattered across my desk. Through the open balcony doors, deep in the sky I saw a distant spaceship, a ball of radiant light, glowing in aura and splendour. I gathered my thoughts and continued working, focused on a special assignment known as Project 8. Along with a team of engineers and astrophysicists, I worked tirelessly, planning the construction of a new city on Mars. The research scientists had laid down the theoretical foundation for the project; it was my duty to coordinate it, hence, making it a reality.

An hour had passed. I needed a break. Walking through the lobby I entered the main office; a glum silence fell, everyone turning towards me, pausing in their work. Moving on, the silence broke; a few comments and faint whispers were exchanged under their breaths.

Lazily I entered the social room and instantly the robot-waitress moved towards me carrying a silver tray of drinks, its relays and memory banks clicking, its life-like eyes dilating. Placing a mug of coffee in my hand, I strolled back to the office, startled by the unnerving behaviour of my work colleagues. Their strange acknowledgement of my presence disturbed me, yet I tried to remain calm and composed. Leaning back against the balcony door I fell into a daze. A peculiar sensation crept over me, almost numbing.

The latter part of the day flashed by. Glancing at my wristwatch I noticed it was now seven o'clock; I was ready to head home. Collating my documents I slid them into my briefcase and rushed to the elevator.

Outside an Mx300 landed to the side of my car; it was one of the many newly designed hover cars. The doors flipped open, steam rising from the bonnet and dissipating into the night mists. Two robot security guards strode towards me, their laser pistols fixed to their belts.

"Good evening, Sir. Just a routine check-up. Can I see your ID card, please?"

Soundlessly I handed it over. The robot held it with his hand-shaped metal gripper. His photocell eyes scanned through it briskly with metallic dignity.

"Sorry to have bothered you, Sir… This complex is like a mini-city, it's impossible to know every face here. Have a good night."

As the Mx300 ascended into the sky, I stepped into my car, heading home. Outside, the city was lifeless; there was an unusual chill in the air. Grey, cold light filled the deserted streets. A few miles ahead lay the city spaceport; a huge steel structure, crafts endlessly ascending, engine emissions floating above.

Arriving home, I pulled into the drive; flashing from the car plasma screen was the day's battery consumption. Steadily I made my way to the door. The security scanner passed over me; with a sharp click the door slid open.

"Jane...? I'm home..."

There was no reply, just the humming sound from the vent unit. Then I heard noise coming from the back room; a clinking of glasses, a stir of motion. Inching my way down the corridor I came towards the living room door. I stood still, dead still... A measure of curiosity came over me.

"Doug, I'm really worried... It seems to be occurring constantly, every night. Michael has changed; I'm getting very concerned."

"Don't worry, Jane. Trust me."

In a burst of fuming rage I flung the door open, storming in. The lights were dim, the side lamp glowing softly in the corner. Jane stood motionless, the colour from her face fading.

"What the hell is going on? What do you think you're playing at, Doug? I can't believe this..."

Jane approached me ominously, placing her hands across my waist, her long coloured lashes flickering nervously.

"Sweetheart, let me explain... I've just been so worried about you. I called Doug and told him to come; I needed to speak to someone. Who better than your best friend? Ever since you started having these nightmares you've been so absent, so withdrawn; your behaviour is so erratic, Michael. It's even affecting your work."

I turned to Doug, who stood there rubbing his forehead.

"Michael, I didn't want to break the news but the management are starting to get concerned. They've noticed a decline in your performance and considering you're working in a very high-profile position, within the biggest engineering company in the world, there's really no room for slacking, regardless of personal problems. Michael, I don't want to sound hard - you're my friend and I do care - but unfortunately, the management see it differently. They may even come to the point of having to make some drastic decisions. I think it would be better for you to tell me what's going on, and what these dreams are about..."

For a moment I paused. Doug stood there staring at me, his face wise with profundity. It was as if he had something concealed behind those staring eyes. I couldn't quite understand why earlier he had so easily dismissed all that I had told him... It didn't seem to equate. I had an odd lingering intuition that something was up... Shifting it aside, I put it down to just a bout of paranoia.

Slowly I walked over to the bar and poured myself a double scotch. *"I know you're thinking I'm losing it, but you must believe me; for the last few weeks I've kept having this dream. In the dream I'm lying in a dark room surrounded by people; people who look like they are preparing to operate on me... In the dream I try hard to scream and move but I can't... Every night it's the same, night after night. Occasionally the characters change but it's always the same dream. You've got to believe me! I can understand having nightmares, but not the same one every night. I can even give you a chronological breakdown of all the events. It's as if..."*

"It's as if what, Michael?"

"It's as if... the dreams were real. I can't explain it; who's to say which is the greater reality: the one we know, or the one in our dreams?"

Jane walked over to me, her face contorted with an expression of discomfort and gloom.

"Michael, look at me."

"You think I'm crazy - don't you? Don't you, Jane?"

"Sweetheart, listen to yourself. I love you but I think you should see someone. These are just silly dreams; you're losing touch with reality. Worrying is only causing you to build up this depression. Baby, you need to come to grips with yourself."

Checking his pocket watch, Doug looked down towards the ground, his shoulders hunched.

"It appears to me you're losing the ability to differentiate between reality and fantasy; between what is and isn't. You've got to start thinking logically with a clear, coherent mind, regardless of your emotions - regardless how real the dreams seem. In a dream a man can live a lifetime but it's all the manufacture of the mind...a created fantasy...a world that doesn't exist. Look, for now I suggest you rest; take a few days off. I'll speak to Professor Franz in the morning..."

Walking up to me, he patted me across my shoulder. With a smile he then turned and headed for the door, his footsteps fading. Jane left the room dejected, the scent of her warm perfume lingering in the air. Dropping into the sofa, I lay there gazing towards the mirrored ceiling, my pale reflection staring back. It was now clear to me: I had to try and fight my fears, my dreams - but how?

Later that night, I was unable to sleep, lying alone on the sofa watching the holographic vision screen. Looking towards the analogue clock my mind began to drift. My eyelids drooped down watching each hour pass, hour after hour ticking by. Slowly my eyes blurred, fatigue rushing in; I began fading, fading away into a deep sleep.

I awoke. It was now 7am. From behind a shadow reflected down against the tiled floor, Jane walked into the living room, holding her bag with one hand, a coffee in the other. She moved around the room as if she was looking for something; it appeared she hadn't noticed me.

"Jane…"

She stood back, gazing over, her face blank and unresponsive.

"How come you're up so early?"

She stuttered and paused, blinking nervously.

"I was wondering where you were. I just thought I'd let you know that I'm going out for the day; I've organised to meet up with Kristen. I told her I'd pick her up around eight…"

"What time will you be back?"

"Not quite sure, I'll give you a call later."

Placing the mug down, she walked away in a hurry, nudging the door closed. Her erratic behaviour was peculiar, to say the least; not quite the bright start to the day I was hoping for.

The day flashed by as I sat alone in front of the holograph, trying to relax my fatigued mind. In a spontaneous burst I decided to head out; sitting alone at home wasn't exactly the best remedy for a depressive state of mind. I changed into some clean clothes, splashing on aftershave. Along the arm of the chair was my jacket; grabbing it, I was on my way.

Driving aimlessly, I suddenly decided to head to work. It was an ideal opportunity for me to speak to Professor Franz myself, an eminent genius whom I had met on the odd occasion. From above, I could hear the sound of hover cars humming softly, their lights flashing across the skyline. Robots were everywhere, moving around in the bustling confusion; in surface cars and balconies, streaming in and out of buildings gossiping. Very few humans were visible, a few standing out between the crowds of metal and plastic in the open air marts, where merchandise from the wealthy colonies of Europa and Mars was sold.

As I passed through the vast array of security checks I entered the car park. Buttoning my jacket, I flipped the car door open, and then stepped out. Ahead of me, clattering against the ground, a group of robot workers moved around the site, their mechanical eyes widening and retracting in continuous motion as they communicated. A few greeted me with a nod of their metal heads; others were unresponsive. After threading by them, I heard a sound; a quick angry buzz of resentment, but for what? A cold chill went up my spine.

Striding on, I arrived at the pyramid-structured skyscraper. The two glass doors slid back as I entered. A beam of red light flashed; it was a security device. Inside the building was an engineering unit where all the robotic machinery was made and modified before being sent to be used in outer space. Feeding my clearance card into the security scanner, the elevator doors slid open. On entry, the plasma screen control panel lit up. I pressed the dial, and began my ascent. Within seconds of my arrival a smartly dressed man approached me, his aged face lined and withered, his eyes like faded blue stones. He stood there gazing at me intuitively.

"Professor Franz has been expecting you. Please come this way."

His voice was monotonous, yet clear. In a moment of confusion I remained silent, following watchfully; obviously, they must have anticipated my arrival. Approaching the office, the man eased his way through the long corridor, clutching his onyx-topped cane. Passing his hand over the laser code detector, the door opened, retracting softly into the wall. To the back of a darkly-lit room stood a mahogany table; behind it sat the Professor, his old faded eyes staring at me as he rose from his chair.

"Michael, don't be bashful... Please come in."

"I'm so sorry to have turned up like this; I know you're a very busy man. I assume Doug must have spoken to you?"

"Here at R.M Special Technologies we have a reputation for producing the finest robotic machinery in the planet. We have built - and are still in the process of building - cities throughout our solar system. People are now able to go on vacations to Mars and Europa. All of this has been made possible through the brilliant minds that we have within this Corporation. You, Michael, are part of it all; an integral asset. Tell me; what seems to be the problem?"

The Professor sat there in his modern immense chair, looking at me profoundly, a delicate smile twitching across his wrinkled, emaciated face. With a heavy hand he parted his dark, thinning hair. A strange thrill shot through me, a peculiar sensation which I couldn't explain.

"Professor, as I'm sure you're aware, I'm in charge of Project 8, and it's requiring a lot of work and energy from me. I don't know quite how to put this; it's kind of strange really, but for the last few weeks I've been having nightmares. The crazy thing is that it's the same one every single night. As a result, my concentration has been affected and I'm not able to work as well. I feel so absent...as if I weren't here. I just can't explain it..."

"Michael, the images in our dreams are influenced by day-to-day events. I'm sure this is just a depressive phase you're experiencing. What I can recommend to you is perhaps to take some time off; or, if you prefer, you can come to work for a couple of hours a day, at least until you feel better."

I was taken aback by the Professor's generous offer; his warm, mild attitude left me at ease, yet somewhat puzzled by his over-accommodating attitude.

"Thank you for your kind consideration. I'll see how things develop throughout the coming weeks."

"Michael, anytime I can be of assistance, please don't hesitate to come and see me."

"Thank you, Professor. I won't take up any more of your time."

That night at the dinner table there was an aura of tension; a hostile atmosphere. Even at home there seemed to be no peace. Jane had hardly exchanged a word throughout the course of the night. In the moments of brief dialogue there was a sullen, uncooperative note in her voice - surely a reflection of things to come. The absence in her eyes troubled me.

Leaving the table I headed straight to bed, alone and tired. The bed lights activated as I strolled in, the mini-robot motionless in the corner. In the bathroom I splashed some warm water across my face and neck. I paused, staring into the rotating mirror. For a split second, it seemed as if the image staring back was an inanimate object; a bizarre sensation. Turning, I reached over for a towel, noticing a gold card lying on the tiled floor. I placed it into the palm of my hand; it read: *'Jane Richards R.M. Special Technologies.'* A chilling premonition moved through me; I was left perplexed. Why did Jane have this card? I had to hold back, refraining from acting impulsively. I needed time to reflect; time to discover more before approaching her. Conversely, I knew whatever was hidden from me would soon surface, but one thing was for certain - something was desperately wrong.

It was early morning when I awoke. Outside it was twilight, the sun's radiance slowly breaking into the darkness as it rose from the horizon. I limped out of bed, my body lame and weak, stripped from its energy. Clearly this psychological facade wasn't exactly helping. Within no time I was dressed. Jane lay asleep, covers pulled and stretched across her body. From the cabinet drawer, I pulled out a bottle of narcotic headache pills, slipping them into my jacket; my head throbbed, aching with pain. Hurriedly, I headed for the door.

In the half-light of dawn, the city began to glow and shimmer. Across the street was a team of inorganic robot child-carers, their undulating arms weaving inquiringly as they communicated with one another. From the apartment blocks a group of teens ran towards them, ready for school.

I sat in my car recapturing my momentum, pondering my next move. From the light transducer the car heated up with brisk effect. Along the dashboard the intercom unit sounded. The screen lit up; Doug's face emerged in ripples of visual static.

"Hi, Michael... I wanted to see how things were going. I called your house - Jane told me you just left..."

"Doug, we need to speak - it's urgent. Can we meet?"

"Sure...regards to?"

"Listen, I can't explain right now!"

For a split second there was silence, the odd crackle.

"I understand. I'll be at work within twenty minutes... Meet me outside in the parking lot."

Swaying through the queues of traffic, I emerged onto the main highway. Peering above I noticed that the sky was condensed with hover cars; air control panels lay fixed against the sidewalk displaying an increase in sky traffic. A line of minicabs came driving by, sounding their car horns; it appeared to be an unusually busy day. All city inhabitants now came into view; endless hundreds, moving feverishly.

Focused on the road, I sped ahead. Before long I was at work, sitting silently in the car park, the window lowered, cold wind sweeping in. My mind was distant, engaged in countless thoughts and theories, none of which enlightened me. Landing in the hover bay, Doug walked out. Instantly I plucked the door open, rushing towards him.

"Doug...! Doug...!"

"Hey, slow down buddy. Tell me what's up?"

"Look... Last night I found this...!"

I placed the card into his hand. Doug stood still, his face expressionless, wide-eyed but composed.

"Did you speak to Jane?"

"No."

"Anyone else?"

"No Doug, no one..."

"Look, with rushing here I forgot to bring some important documents...I have to go back to the apartment. Why don't you jump in?"

Without reply I sat inside the hover car, latching the security belt across my chest. Gravitating above the ground we slowly ascended into the atmosphere, disappearing into clouds of vapour. I rested my head against the window and gazed down below, captivated by the bright flickering lights coming from the city skyscrapers. Suddenly the sky darkened and within a short time there was a severe rainstorm. Formless dark clouds filled the surrounding air, stretching into the stratosphere, faint glimpses of blue sky appearing between breaks in the cloud deck. Flicking through the control dials, Doug engaged the autopilot. Releasing his security belt he turned to me.

"Michael... I can understand how you're feeling. I'll give you my theory for what it's worth... I mean, it is bizarre but I'm sure there's a rational explanation for it all. Perhaps the Corporation gave her the card because of you; after all, you are one of the leading engineers within the establishment, one of the top guys..."

As I sat absorbing the words that came from Doug, I was unconvinced by his frail attempt to justify an obviously perplexing scenario. There seemed to be an inconsistency in his character and a weak point in his logic. The only way to relieve the anxiety that was mounting within me was to challenge her; it was the obvious solution. Before I could even mutter a word we began our descent, the hover car tilting violently from side to side as the wind intensified, control dials springing into life displaying a radical change in atmospheric pressure. Within minutes we were on the ground, parked to the side of a skyscraper.

"Michael, why don't you come up with me? I'll fix you a stiff drink."

As we stood in the elevator ascending to the 90th floor, I glanced towards Doug as he casually lit his cigarette. He seemed agitated and worried as he puffed away, biting the edges of his mouth; something was on his mind.

Entering the apartment, Doug walked over to the far end of the room. The sofa was littered with papers and documents, which seemed to be of no importance to him, as he shifted them to one side.

"So Michael, what can I get you? The usual?"

"Yeah... A double scotch would be nice."

Turning to the window I glanced at the magnificent metropolis down below. The view was mildly obscured by the rain and a hazy mist which was now engulfing the city. I paused, watching the rain fall from the sky, endless torrents showering down. My eyes became somewhat captivated; my mind began to ease, drifting away. A sudden tug against my shoulder broke my concentration.

"Here you go, Michael. Knock that back."

Placing the glass on the table, he then slipped out of his jacket, walking towards the corridor. As I sat on the sofa sipping my drink I felt as if I was caught up in some kind of imaginary web; as if I was losing touch with reality.

As for Jane, I had no answers... As I searched my mind it became all the more clear. The woman I was married to was not who I thought she was. Resting back against the sofa, the room was silent and still but for the sound of the restless rain beating down on the large balcony window. Then I heard footsteps. Doug walked in clutching a steel briefcase.

"Michael, I just received a text; I need to rush back to work urgently. Why don't you stay here? The change of ambience will do you good."

For a moment I sat in contemplation. After a few brief seconds I decided that going to work was best; perhaps there were other hidden realities to be explored, ones that could help piece together this baffling puzzle.

"Thanks, Doug, but I think I'll come to work. Besides, my car's there."

Grabbing his jacket, we were on our way.

Back at the office I sat at my desk, sipping a cup of warm coffee. A sudden knock at the door disturbed my thoughts. Before I could respond the door opened. A tall bald man entered, a folder under his arm. His neck was long and the cords stood out from his pale wrinkled skin.

"Sorry to disturb you. I'm Professor Leyland. May I take a seat?"

"Sure, go ahead... I don't believe we've met."

"Indeed we haven't..."

As he went to sit down he pulled out a document from his folder. The document contained highly complex mathematical diagrams and calculations. Removing his steel-rimmed specs, he placed them into a silver coloured case. Turning to me, he smiled.

"You're probably wondering what this is all about, Michael. Firstly, in case you're not aware, my role at R.M Special Technologies is to monitor and run various health tests on all the personnel that work for the corporation; especially on individuals who have been working in outer space for long periods. Hence, the nature of my visit is to discuss - and this is purely optional - the possibility of running a series of tests on you, taking into account that you have been suffering, from what I have been told, a severe depression. Professor Franz has personally suggested to me that it's the best avenue to take, given that we have some very highly developed medication available to us. Once the tests have been completed successfully, it will enable us to take things further."

For a moment I didn't know how to reply. One thing was for sure; Professor Leyland's suave, eloquent approach did make me think. He seemed deeply concerned as he sat there looking at me intently.

"Okay, Professor. When would you want to run these tests on me?"

"Later today would be perfect, Michael. Let's say 6pm. I'm located in section 25-D, on the fiftieth floor. I look forward to it."

As he left the office I walked over towards the balcony, shifting the glass doors apart. The rain had ceased, yet the sky was still dull and cloudy. The hazy mist which had engulfed the city a few hours before caused the surrounding air to become moist. Resting my hand against my forehead, I fell into a daze, staring into the void.

It was now six o'clock and I was heading towards Professor Leyland's office. Outside it was dark, the occasional glare of light passing by from rotating motion detectors. Approaching the elevator I slipped out my clearance card, feeding it into the security scanner. Instantly the doors slid open and I began my ascent. Reaching the fiftieth floor, the elevator stopped. The voice box bleeped into life; a robotic voice recording followed, fine and metallic.

'Please read out your security number.'

'RM8-3855X.'

The elevator doors slowly opened. Walking out I entered a large reception area. From beyond a winding corridor a young woman approached me; there was something magnetic about her. Her delicate smile and sense of wellbeing helped me to deflect away from my fears and anxieties.

"You must be Michael Richards. I'm Adina. Professor Leyland has been expecting you... Please come this way."

I shook her hand. Her eyes were sparkling bright, her perfume warm sweet and tantalising, her lips twisting into a pout. Within seconds I was led into a dimly-lit room, cool ventilated air blowing around me. The room was filled with a vast array of computers and machinery, highly complex equipment. In a corner stood a lifeless robot, its slender metallic frame shining under an overhead light. From its panelled breastplate I could hear faint sounds of the delivery drum winding up memory tape as it circulated, activating its mechanical nervous system. It was a basic model, one of the very first made; one which I had worked with in times past.

These particular models were subject to infinite realities; simply by changing its memory roll its identity could be altered. On a glass table was a set of robot arms, covered in a baffling maze of circuitry. From behind I felt a cold hand dig into my shoulder.

"Hi, Michael. I see you've taken a liking to my robot. It's being used within one of our laboratories for specific tasks; its voice box is yet to be modified, it's still fine and metallic."

He stood smiling, fixing his tie.

"Michael, please make yourself comfortable. Oh - before we begin, this is my assistant Doctor Newville; he's just got back from a space cruise."

"It's good to meet you, Michael."

A serene smile spread over his face; it appeared to be manufactured. Almost instantly, I recalled that he was one of the characters in my dream. The obvious surprise startled me, as I tried desperately to refrain from acting impulsively. The next thing I knew, I was led to a hygienic bed. Positioned on either side stood two large machines constructed from various alloys. Above my head an X-ray device was lowered, on top lay what looked like a small prism. From the prism a spectrum of colours shone, glittering with burning intensity from no apparent source. As the machine activated into life, it released sounds like fluctuating pulses. The Professor leaned over, peering down acutely into my face.

"Michael, I'm going to give you a vaccination. It's going to sedate you... Lie back... Close your eyes."

"Why a vaccination?"

"Trust me, Michael."

As he inserted a large syringe into my arm, a sequence of images began to surge through my mind, pictures of my life flashing before me. My torso suddenly became rigid and hard, the vaccine leaving me in a paralytic state. There was a feeling in me that my body had become the manifestation of some uncontrollable power, as if I had become a non-being. A reflex spasm of the optic nerve shifted my eyes open violently; my vision blurred, fading and receding. Glancing around the room, all the images now appeared distorted. Through the small narrow window the moon had become an elongated sphere, rolling and twisting in the emptiness of space. With a wave of dizziness my eyes closed tightly... I could dimly hear a voice.

"He's well under sedation now... He seems to have reacted well to the idrodine."

Next, I awoke lying on the bed; my face heavily perspiring, an acute pain rippling through my left arm. The room was warm and empty, tinged with the smell of chemicals. From the corridor I heard faint footsteps, a murmur of voices in the background. The Professor walked in, a gleeful grin broadening across his face.

"Michael, you're finally up. Tell me, how're you feeling?"

For a moment I didn't reply, my voice was dull - drug-saturated.

"Professor, I have to say I had some really odd experiences. I can't recall much... but what I can remember was this feeling of separation from reality... I just can't explain it."

91

"These emotions and feelings can be generated as a result of the high dosages of drugs that I had to administer during the tests. Don't worry, as soon as we're ready, I'll get back to you with the results. As for now, you're free to leave."

"Professor...just one thing before I go...?"

Placing his clipboard and pen on the table, he stood staring at me.

"Tell me, why has there been so much attention focused on my situation; why so much effort from the Corporation?"

The Professor seemed taken aback by my questioning, as if there was some other hidden motive, one he wasn't prepared to disclose.

"Michael, as I have already explained, it's the Corporation's duty to see that all personnel are taken care of and monitored - you yourself know the troubles you've been experiencing. Think nothing more of it. Come, get your things together, and when you get back see to it that you get some much-needed rest."

Gathering my thoughts, I was unconvinced by his dismissive attitude. It appeared as if he was preoccupied with another matter. I decided to kill the discussion there. Making my way to the elevator, my body was still numb and weak, my head and vision somewhat blurred.

It was 9pm. I was on my way home, guided expertly by the autonomic circuit, the dashboard lights coming into focus and flickering as I regulated the glow-dial. The evening air was thin and crisp; the moonlight diffused a pale illumination which shone down, reflecting against the road. The highway was empty; the city quiet and still. Descending spacecraft broke the evening silence as they swept relentlessly overhead. After a short time the autopilot began to disengage. I was minutes from home; it was now time to confront Jane.

Arriving, I noticed that the house was dark, but for the outside ground lights. Steadily I rushed in.

"Hello, Jane...?"

There was no reply. The atmosphere in the house was tense, the silence unnerving. She should have been back hours ago. Kneeling down, I began to wonder... At that moment there was a loud knock. Anxiously I walked over to the door.

"Hi..."

"Mind if I come in?"

"Sure, Doug. Tell me, do you have any idea where Jane is?"

He hesitated. His lack of response troubled me. Walking into the living room he seemed despondent, a mysterious expression of concealment glowing across his face. From the bar he fixed himself a drink, his hands shaking nervously as he sipped at it.

"Doug, are you okay? Problems at the office?"

"No, Michael...just busy organising things. A group of workers in our section have been transferred; they're leaving for Europa. They're also sending a new team to Mars, for the exploration of the underground mines."

As Doug sank into the armchair he rubbed his forehead, knocking back his drink. It seemed he was preparing to tell me something. A look of sadness permeated out from his staring eyes; for a moment they appeared to have a polished, inorganic quality about them.

"Doug, what is it? Tell me!"

He placed the empty glass on the table. There was a strange, granite cast to his face; an unusual hardness. I stood still, gripped with an element of expectancy.

"Michael, before long I will be sent away, just like all of us, to work in the harsh, hazardous environments of one of our neighbouring planets. This is why we were built; this is what you were made for..."

"What are you saying...?"

"Can't you see, Michael? R.M Special Technologies needed people to work in outer space... They required labourers to work in the harsh environments of Mars and Europa; without us they would have never accomplished all that we see today. Do you really believe that they constructed all those elaborate space cities...?

"We were the ones who built and designed them... It was us humanoids who were responsible for melting the ice caps on Mars; it was us who built the endless pipe lines blowing oxygen into the carbon dioxide-ridden atmosphere...

"Humanoids have changed the cosmos. No humans were prepared to sacrifice themselves; it was far too dangerous for them to live and work on those planets... In spite of all the technological know-how, man could never adapt to such hostile worlds. The long-term physiological effects on a human, or any organic life form, were potentially fatal, as you are well aware - not to mention the constant bombardment of gamma rays; radiation from supernovae, the absence of the Earth's gravitational field all proved too much. This was why they constructed us, as a result of their hunger to colonise the solar system, to quench that innate burning desire to conquer the stars... We were programmed, finely tuned with human-like emotions and desires; a mental capacity to make decisions within a set scope. There's a grid screen, a matrix implanted within us which cuts us off from certain thought patterns and actions. It interferes with the wave frequency which would otherwise give us total freedom..."

"Are you saying we are computerised machines? Have you lost your mind?"

"Aside from the Management, we, and everyone at R.M Special Technologies, are humanoids, built from flesh and machine; biomechanical, a mass of intricate wires, electrodes and flesh, finely put together. But you were the newest, the finest prototype to

be built. You are a top level robot, unlike us ordinary flesh and metal-limbed workers, made more human than human; built with a life memory with a distinctive life history and evolution. From my first breath of life I was aware of my function, and what I am; a brutal reality. This has been suppressed deep inside me for years; what you are has remained dormant within you till now. All I have ever wanted was to gain true homeostatic function, but I could never achieve this; indeed, none of us could or can. Perhaps locating and then manipulating the programming circuit could give us independent thought and function - homeostatic function, control of our reality, our destiny... "

"But how...? How can this be? I can remember my whole life from when I was a child, every little intricate detail..."

"It's all synthetically programmed, an electric fantasy - an artificial construct giving you the illusion of being in control and real. We have never been in control... the only difference now is that you are aware."

"Are you suggesting that my whole existence subsists in a small chip implanted in my head?"

"Your memories are nothing more than an artificial implant, false recall. Your function was a simple one: to gain as much knowledge and practical expertise on Earth before your permanent transfer to outer space. You were the ultimate humanoid, which would lead man into the depths of space and beyond...As for Jane, she works with the Corporation. She was part of the project. This is why you found the card; she was appointed as your wife. I had no choice but to lie to you, and conceal the truth - it was imposed on me. When the Corporation realised that you began to suspect, they knew that their project hadn't gone to plan - the very tests you just took confirm this. Building a humanoid of your stature was to prove their undoing. It was only a matter of time before you were going to discover this life-changing truth. Your dreams were nothing more than reliving a past memory; somehow in your psyche you had recaptured the point in time of your construction."

"No, I'm real... I'm not a machine, I'm physical... My destiny lies in my hands; I'm in control of my thoughts and desires... I'm not bound by mechanical emotions and sensations...!"

In a flash, everything around me twisted into a blur fading off into obscurity, the colours in the room draining away, filmed in a haze of darkness. I fell back onto the sofa squinting, barely making out the faint image of Doug, the analogue clock ticking loudly. A string of sounds rattled from within me, the sound of fusing circuit boards, and dying machinery. Opening my mouth, I went to speak, but no words would come. Ripples of my life surged through my mind, with it sensations and forgotten emotions. I could feel the wind blowing over me; I could see colourful birds gliding graciously through the air... butterflies...lively creatures...elaborate landscapes, cascading falls...

I was lost, lost in a haze of relative existence.

"Michael, you cannot bypass the stark reality of what is. My objective for being here was to tell you that the Corporation has made a decision. You're going to be modified; rebuilt from scratch, re-implanted with a new memory. As we speak you're shutting down; Professor Leyland triggered off the process. You have been living a delusion Michael, a delusion behind mechanical eyes; a delusion of being human and alive. Every humanoid has its expiry date..."

I pulled the bed sheets aside, flicking on the light switch; my heart beating, my face heavily perspiring.

"Ed, honey, are you okay?"

"Yes Jane, just a nightmare..."

Chronology

THEY descended onto an arid landscape. A strong gust of dry wind swept against the spacecraft, brushing particles of sand into the open atmosphere. Colonel Rick Harrington, scientist and astronaut, had just returned from his final space mission along with his co-pilot. On their return to Earth, all seemed normal...

Yanking the steel lever, the hydraulic powered doors shifted apart. Walking out, they found themselves stranded in an isolated desert. Above, the scorching sun glowed as it hung high in the distance, its rays beaming with intense heat.

"That was close... we nearly lost all power. Where are we?"

"Planet Earth, I hope!" Rick chuckled vacantly, *"This has to be the Mojave Desert... At least, that's what the navigation system was indicating. Hold tight, Sebastian; the rescue team will be here within no time."*

As Rick pulled off his lead-lined space helmet his face dripped with sweat, his view-plate steamed with moisture. Glancing into the distance, the mere thought of being left in the desert was unthinkable. Ahead lay endless miles of burning sand, an arid world where life survives against terrifying odds. Opening his bottled water, which was fixed to his belt, he quenched his thirst.

"Damn it, Rick, I can't seem to get any contact with the control tower..."

Rick was unresponsive, somewhat captivated by the landscape; his eyes were fixed curiously towards the arid wilderness, his white spacesuit shining faintly in the blazing desert sun. Raising his transmitter to his lips, he attempted to contact the control tower.

"Control tower...this is Explorer 255, do you copy? Hello, control tower...?"

For a moment there was a voice, faint and distant; almost lost in the static. Silence followed. Rick clicked off the transmitter and returned it to his belt. Throwing his helmet into the sand, he grew agitated; fatigue soon crept in. Taking a deep breath, he filled his lungs with humid air. The burning heat was stifling, the humidity unbearable. Even the occasional gust of wind was unable to cool him. Pulling off his oxygen tank, windblown sand whipped against him. Walking over, Sebastian held his canister, splashing water across his perspiring face.

"It's probably best if we go back inside the spacecraft...keep in the shade. Looks like we will have to wait a while for the rescue team..."

Under a blood red sky the sun was setting in the horizon, a suspended orb shimmering in the far-off distance. As nightfall approached the temperature radically changed; a cool breeze filled the desert air, vast billowing clouds of sand and dust blowing endlessly over the wilderness. A cluster of stars sparkled stretching across the sky, radiating light throughout the stratosphere. Inside the spacecraft, Rick and Sebastian lay awake. It was still; an ominous silence throughout.

"Rick, are you still up?"

"Yeah, can't seem to get any sleep."

"What do you think's happening? I mean, the rescue team should have been here hours ago... At the very least, they should have radioed in... We've heard absolutely nothing!"

Rick remained silent, running his hand across his forehead, searching his mind for logical answers.

"Odd... No communication with us whatsoever. When I tried to contact the control tower all I was getting was static...wave interference."

"We're running out of water supplies. It's vital we keep hydrated in these conditions... We won't last long, Rick."

"I know. For now, try to get some rest... We need to conserve as much energy as possible."

At the crack of dawn sunlight filled the sky, blinding and hot. Opening the doors, they walked out. No signs of life, just the barren wilderness, empty and void. Suddenly from the sky a radiant bolt of light crashed down, sweeping desert sand into the air. A lizard slithered away, concealing itself.

"What was that?"

Sebastian was speechless, rigid; his eyes wandering as he glanced into the blue. In perpetual motion a string of lights fell, consuming a large rock into tiny fragments. Rick lost his balance, stumbling into the burning sand. Slashed across the sky was a trail of dense grey smoke; a spaceship hovered, moving sporadically from side to side. The ship then shuddered as it polarised into position, releasing another glowing beam of light which fell towards Rick as he lay there in awe. Sebastian edged over, reaching out his hand.

"Quick, into the craft! We've got to get out of here!"

Before they could move, the light beam swirled around them, lifting them high above the ground towards an opening in the ship. Entering, they were lowered into a small luminous dome which was lined with a reddish haze.

Left in a daze, Rick leapt to his feet, his boots filled with desert dust. For a moment there was an astonished silence.

"What happened? Where are we?"

"I don't know," Sebastian replied.

As the rays slowly faded, a tall dignified figure of a man entered into the dome. His face was emaciated with defined features, his eyes a pale green, almost without colour. With a sharp, penetrating voice he spoke out.

"Welcome to Earth! From where have you come?"

Regaining his composure, Rick cautiously moved towards him, a cold alarm plucking at him.

"What do you mean, 'welcome to Earth'? Who are you? How did we get here? When we left Earth…"

The man's commanding tone quickly drowned out his words.

"Earth… Only the Specialised Forces are allowed to leave Earth. Once we finished colonising our solar system, space has hardly been touched. Life can only be sustained here. Our voyages into space were nothing more than conquering the unknown…"

It went silent. Before Rick could reply, the man walked away, his boots squeaking against the rubbery surface. Instantly the luminous rays reactivated, securing the dome. Slowly, Rick began to recall what had happened.

The huge ship roared on, passing through a dense cloud belt, coasting over the surface of the land that stretched as far as the eye could see. A city came into view; an ocean, dark and miserable, water lapping below, crusted with salt and debris. As the ship shuddered it reduced velocity manoeuvring for descent towards a gigantic spaceport, endless flickering towers, buildings and landways. On touchdown the ground rumbled under them violently - then silence. Above, the sky was filled with radioactive particles, beta and gamma rays; a reminder to all of the nuclear war which had once threatened to obliterate mankind. The hard radiation had brought mutation at all levels; insects, plants and animals.

As the rays deactivated, a group of soldiers stormed into the glowing dome. Behind stood a robot, built from twisted steel; highly developed circuits and intricate wires.

In its grippers it held a document and pen expertly, its photocell eyes staring menacingly. A faint sheen of distaste spread across its features.

Pointing their blast guns, the soldiers led Rick out of the ship down a ramp; Sebastian following close behind. Outside there was a torrent of sounds and confusion; spaceport officials hurrying around energetically. Workmen began to congregate around the spaceship inspecting. Looking over, Rick noticed an old building, one which jerked his memory. Once part of the old LAX airport, it now stood as an old ruin, an eclipse of the past. Above the spaceport, in the form of a hologram were the words: 'WELCOME TO LOS ANGELES YEAR 3002.'

"Sebastian, look - it can't be...!"

Sebastian stood in awe, his mind thrown into oblivion, sweat dripping from his face and neck. His eyes spoke clearer than words; his face a manifestation of horror and mystification. They had returned to a new world where hundreds of years had elapsed; a world which had radically changed. Gazing around, Rick fought down rising terror; a profound caution had gripped him inwardly.

From an opening in the spaceport, a military glider advanced, its engines roaring violently, its metallic aerodynamic shaped frame glittering in the blazing sun. Slowly it came to a halt, stopping beside the ship. With a faint hum the doors retracted. Inside lay a vacant chamber; at the front, driving, sat two armed soldiers. With a heavy shove to the back Sebastian fell to the ground. Rick turned, looking at the group of soldiers, burning with anger - a controlled anger.

"Why are you treating us like this? What are you people?"

A soldier walked over, pointing his blast gun.

"You're not in the position to ask questions. Get into the truck... NOW!"

The commanding sound of his voice rose wildly over the roar of the engines.

Hurriedly they moved in. With a sharp click the doors shut tight, the bolts fell into place and the glider began to move away, gaining speed. Peering from a narrow barred window, Rick caught glimpses of the city ahead, awed by what he saw. It appeared to be constructed from a crystallised material, no longer resembling the one he had left behind. The magnificent metropolis was glowing yellow from the sun, bursting and thriving with human life. Soaring high above the city stood a spectacular dome-shaped skyscraper, immense in diameter. Fixed above it was a rotating radar emitting pulses of light. It was used to locate the positioning of spacecraft; ones that travelled throughout the cosmos. Housed inside the dome was a miniature town complex which had been constructed after the initial blast to protect the city folk from the radioactive particles which covered the Earth.

His eyes wearily absorbed the scene; his mind began to drift. Turning to Sebastian, he passed his hand across his forehead.

"Sebastian, somehow we have been catapulted ahead in time. Hundreds of years have elapsed... Do you recall as we entered the Earth's atmosphere there was a

blinding light; seconds later it passed? Perhaps somewhere between the sky and Earth lies a doorway - perhaps to another dimension - one parallel to our own. The universe is complex, Sebastian; made up of sub-atomic particles, strings of light oscillating with a frequency of which we are all part; a symphony of sounds within a multiverse of parallel dimensions, infinite realities."

The military glider began losing speed, stopping outside a line of buildings, its powerful engines ceasing into silence. As the doors slid open a group of soldiers stood waiting, swarming around. Rick walked out, Sebastian following behind. They were forced into a building, and then led into a confined room covered by a stone floor.

Gazing around, Rick noticed that the room was totally sealed off, closed in by thick titanium walls. He paused. Frustrated anger threatened to overwhelm him. Across, sitting at the back of a large translucent table, was a voluptuous woman, well-groomed with piercing green eyes. Her official uniform was an indication that she was there to interrogate and conduct an investigation. Rick was intrigued by the woman, her delicate soft eyes camouflaging something more sinister; it lured him into a false sense of security. He studied her; the expression on her face, the faint motion of her lips.

"Allow me to introduce myself. I'm Yespa, I work with the Special Forces. I hear that you were both found stranded in the desert."

Waving her hand, an immense map glowed into existence before them; it pictured the precise location of their descent into the Mojave Desert with startling accuracy. The edges of the map faded off into obscurity. Rick caught his breath. He saw an infinite web of detailed sections; a network of squares and lines, glowing green and blue. Clearing her throat, she resumed discussion.

"Tell me, which planet are you from?"

The map wavered and changed, picturing the solar system, all the planets orbiting around the sun, a brilliant vivid luminous image. Rick despondently turned his head to the floor, his eyes glazed and set with confusion. Before Sebastian could reply, he interrupted, his husky voice rising in anger, his palate sour, sapped of its moisture.

"Planet? I'm a human; not an alien. What is this? Are you people mad? The reason why we were in the desert was because we had to make an emergency landing; we had just returned from a space mission. I just don't know how or what has happened. We left Earth only a few months ago; it now seems we have returned to another world - another time..."

The woman was expressionless and unresponsive. The map faded off. Raising her finger, she pointed it towards him.

"For years, we humans believed that the cosmos was lifeless. Indeed, after hundreds of visits to other planets, we never found anything - but your arrival on Earth suggests different."

Rick clenched his fist in anger.

"Are you telling me you believe that I'm an alien? Do I look like one?"

A cold grin broadened across her face, almost cynical, fading moments later.

"Who's to say that aliens don't resemble humans? Your physiology - the way you are structured - doesn't remove that possibility...the possibility that you are from another world. However, these are the accusations against you both."

"Accusations!" Rick stood in disbelief.

"The Operating Commander will be arriving shortly; he will decide your fate."

Rick felt powerless, trapped in this chronological chaos. Not only had they returned to Earth in another time, but they were not even recognised amongst their own. Rising from her chair, the woman walked around the room; her arms crossed, her pointed boots scraping on the stone floor. A brief silence followed. Sebastian remained speechless, wiping nervous sweat from his lips and forehead. A sudden thump against the door broke the silence. Entering the room was the Operating Commander, his long military jacket dragging behind him. A feeling of superiority oozed from his being; his steadfast walk and fixed look emphasising the measure of his confidence. Clutching his cased hand gun, he sat observing.

"In case you are not aware, I'm one of the Commanders. I was instructed to tell you that you will both be taken to the Terra Base prison where you will be detained and interrogated at great length. Your spacecraft has been taken in for examination. I must say it's quite an artefact - unlike what we would have expected from an advanced civilisation. Tell me, from where have you come...and why are you here? Are you spies, alien spies? These are the allegations against you. I hope you understand the implications - do you?"

Overladen with burning, uncontrollable rage, Rick threw his fist against the translucent table, the cords in his neck rippling with anger.

"You people are crazy... Crazy!"

A group of soldiers then stormed in, pulling Sebastian away; dragging him across the stone floor. Turning, Rick felt a cold hand digging into his shoulder. He yelled, throwing his fists violently. It was no use; his cries and moans were in vain, drowned out in the chaos. The Commander rose to his feet.

"Take them away – quickly, into the glider."

Outside, the glider gravitated above the ground. This time a different destination awaited them; it appeared that their fate was now marked. Moving in, Rick lay against the cold steel floor, a look of exhaustion in his eyes. Next to him Sebastian sat rubbing his jaw reflectively. Endless thoughts and images flashed through his mind. He recalled the Earth as it once was; the twisting, blurring images of his wife and friends followed…the scenes then dissolving almost as quickly as they had come.

A whiff of hot air entered through the barred window; a wall of sound struck him. Rick awoke, his reflection scattered across the shiny ceiling; a dazzle of reflected sunlight stinging his eyes. As he pulled himself up, he glanced through the window, staring towards the sea; he could hear it swishing. The ocean's surface was not the spectacle he recalled; boundless miles of foaming dirt-ridden water tossed to and fro, waves crashing furiously against the rocky shore line, leaving a rotten salty stench in the air.

Scattered above was a flock of seagulls gliding graciously through the biosphere; it caused his mind to reflect back to times past. Suddenly he was distracted, his attention momentarily deflected by a huge steel structure which stood far out, in deep water. It was used for absorbing minerals from the ocean such as limestone; minerals which had now become scarce.

From behind, bolted inside an old speed tank, a gang of rebel mutants followed the military glider with one intention. They were the outcasts - a community of people abandoned by the world. Inside, corrosion had eaten away at large sections of the tank; rusty metal machinery sank into decay, dials cracked and broken. Nestled in a small control chamber, the mutants were preparing to fire a laser gun at the glider. Gripping the controls, they directed the tank nozzle, releasing the firing button. With a loud shrilling sound, a string of lasers fired out, igniting in the air. On impact the glider lost control, its bombproof walls preventing it from blowing.

"Sebastian, wake up!"

"What's going on?"

"I'm not quite sure… Quick, prepare yourself - I think we're going to crash."

Rapidly the glider lost speed and momentum, scraping heavily against the ground, showering sparks into the sky. Clutching the wheel frantically, one of the soldiers tried to regain control. He pulled the hover throttle but it failed to respond. Finally it lost power, rolling towards an empty beach, pelting fiercely into the sand. Silence fell; the only sounds coming from the breaking waves and flowing sea water. Disappearing into the distance, the mutants left the site.

Lying there motionless, Rick opened his eyes, his vision blurred by thick smoke. In a daze he looked over, noticing the lifeless body of Sebastian. Gently he slid over, his face alive with hope. Pulling himself through the rubble, he detected a faint heartbeat.

"Sebastian… Sebastian, can you hear me?"

Opening his eyes, he looked up, dimly conscious; his face pale, lips twitching uncontrollably.

"Rick… I don't know if I can make it… Leave me behind," he mumbled with a dull voice.

"There's no way - you're coming with me!"

Gripping him by the arm, Rick gently pulled him out of the wreckage, his feet sinking into the sand. Outside, darkness was descending, falling above the Pacific. Rushing to the front of the glider, Rick saw the two soldiers lying there still; there appeared to be no signs of life. Moving in, he armed himself with a laser pistol, securing it to his belt. Suddenly a strong glaring light shone towards the wreckage. Up ahead on the road was a team of soldiers seated in a large military glider truck. Holding his breath, he rushed over to Sebastian, dragging him through the sand.

"Rick, they'll get us both… Run… Run!"

A ripple of pain burst loose inside him; he groaned in agony. As the glider truck arrived, the team of soldiers stormed out, their blast guns latched loosely across their chests. Instantly Rick ran, concealing himself behind an old wooden beach hut, puffing and red-faced, his line of footprints dimly visible in the sand. The wood was dry and cracked; there was an odour of age and dust. Looking over he saw Sebastian being pulled away, dragged towards the road. Sounds of chatter and confusion resonated through the gloom. Rick lay silent, swallowing with a dry throat. Old memories flooded his mind; unwanted tears burned in his eyes. Sidling through a broken window, he entered the vacant beach hut. Scrambling to his feet he stood gazing, his chest rising and falling as he regained his breath. *How is this possible?* he asked himself, breaking down into a fit of nervous laughter and mounting hysteria.

After a solemn pause, he began recapturing his composure. Scanning the hut he heard a sound. Above a small desk he noticed an archaic fan humming softly, accumulated dust particles circulating around it. Sprawled across the wooden floor lay a broken lantern; fixed to the wall was a stuffed bird, age eating away at it. A sudden bout of exhaustion burst loose within him. He sank down to the ground, his right foot breaking through the weak floorboards.

With ease he managed to pull it out from the yawning, jagged hole. Within minutes he was asleep.

The sound of squalling seagulls and burning sunlight awoke him. Opening his eyes, the sun's rays filtered in through the broken window. The air was parched; stripped dry, almost intolerable. Dazed, he lay observing, his mind switching back into the rhythm of the unfolding events. Lifting himself from the ground, he moved to the door, loose cracked floorboards creaking as he made his way over. With immense effort and strain he pulled the tilting door open, his muscles flexing as it dragged across the wooden floor. Walking out, he glanced around with caution in a somewhat weary motion, the sun glowing in his eyes. The beach was empty; wet with ocean spray, the road bare, no one in sight. His imagination wandered, envisaging what lay ahead. Images of his family lay vividly in his mind; the overwhelming desire to see them again gripped him with agonising pain.

Rushing to the road, Rick decided to head to the city. He moved blindly, without purpose; lost in a haze of confusion and fear like an abandoned fugitive with no fixed direction. All he had left was the desire to stay alive, hoping to find Sebastian - but where would he find him? *Maybe at the Terra Base prison,* he thought to himself bitterly. Yet he knew there was no way of getting there - at least, not now. His eyes roamed wildly, seeing an unending path and an arid landscape ahead; rocks, sand and dust, searing heat.

Slowly, he walked south, down the Pacific coast; windblown particles sweeping around him. Squinting, he staggered on, as if wading through shifting sand; his feet burned and ached. His face was drenched with sweat; his eyes bloodshot red. The effects of dehydration slowly began to set in - he desperately needed water. As he halted, pausing for breath, he heard a sound - roaring engines. In a blur he looked forward. Hurling towards him was a gang of mutants riding on motorbikes. He stood motionless without expression, his lips dry and cracked, bitter lines irritating the sides of his mouth. Slowing down, they stopped, studying him with growing interest. Their ripped sleeves were rolled up, exposing rippling gleaming muscles, dripping with hot sweat. Rick stepped back gripped with panic; their physiology was somewhat diverse to that of regular human beings.

The mutants were abnormally short, with a coarse reddish dark pigment. Their eyes were curious and heavy-lidded, their noses broad and flat; hair like thick dark filaments. For hundreds of years the sun had beaten mercilessly down on them; a horde of radiation-saturated beings.

"Who are you?" grumbled one of the mutants.

After a brief interval of silence, Rick bravely replied.

"Please, I mean no harm... Look, I need help..."

They gazed at each other; it was obvious to them he posed no threat.

"Where are you heading?"

"The city."

"Come... We'll give you a ride."

Rick was anxious, uncertain of their intentions. After a moment of contemplation, he walked over towards the gang of mutants and sat to the back of a motorbike. In a loud burst of speed they stormed away in unison, darting into the distance, Rick gripping the handlebar from behind for support. Nearing the city he noticed a tall building. Its elaborate frame was constructed from some kind of fluorescent metal; an artefact from an advanced culture. At last they had arrived, stopping on the outskirts of the city. An odour of rotten waste lingered in the air, waves of hard radiation drifting above the sky. Stepping from the motorbike, Rick reached over to the mutant, shaking his leather-like hand, gravel crunching under his boots.

"Mind how you go, mister. Here - you'll probably need this."

From a shoulder bag, the mutant pulled out a canister filled with water. He tossed it towards him; Rick grabbed it.

"Thanks," he muttered with a broken, dried-out voice, eyes full of surprise.

Without reply they turned, riding away in the direction of the coast. Rick was alone, uncertain of where to go. Gazing around, he looked over his shoulder. The path seemed clear; no one in sight, but for a few drunkards lying in the afternoon sun. Opening the canister, he drank, pouring the water down hurriedly, sprinkling the remaining drops across his face. Rick halted for a brief moment, regaining his breath, then commenced a slow, cautious walk towards the city. Shakily he checked for his laser pistol, keeping it within his reach. The thought of using it troubled him. Ahead he saw towering structures; peculiar-shaped buildings. Everything seemed somewhat familiar to him in an oddly distorted way; after all, the city was once home to him...*centuries ago.* Then, from seemingly nowhere, he saw a group of soldiers. With immediate action he raced towards a parked glider, concealing himself. He was silent, shifting his eyes nervously, calculating his next move. From behind, a door swung open as a gush of wind swept by.

He turned glancing over. A building - an abandoned building. Dashing over, he entered. Shards of broken glass and old rags lay sprawled on the ground; dirt and graffiti slashed across the walls. Hurriedly he made his way up a flight of steps, three at a time, gripping onto a rusty banister.

Reaching the second level he noticed a door. Moving over, he pushed it open effortlessly and then entered. The apartment appeared uninhabited, soundless but for a dripping tap. The air was rancid, a smell of dung commingling with the heat of the early afternoon. Reaching for the laser pistol, he began a slow, cautious walk down the corridor, his face choked with revulsion. Old floorboards creaked and gave way.

On either side, the walls were streaked with water stains, stripped and cracked; an old oil painting hung half-dangling, covered in what looked like a pulverised chalk. Inching his way in slowly, he entered the bedroom, his vision mildly obscured by dust. Jet-black curtains covered a small window, darkening the room. To the side lay a bed, sheet covers torn and spread apart. A long grey umbrella lay resting on the floor, a pool of sticky water around its shiny metal point. Suddenly a holographic image appeared before him. Instantly he raised the pistol, gripping it tightly with both hands. The image projected vivid scenes of the war from a rectangular metal box which hung fixed to the wall. Other scenes followed; robots building cities, clearing debris left from the battle. Rick was fascinated, staring in wonder. Moving closer, the images appeared to oscillate, slowly fading before him.

Guided by his curiosity, he began to inspect the room. Opening a wardrobe, he found a pile of clothes tied in a brown cord; to the side, leather shoes. Reaching over, he began changing from his sweat-drenched spacesuit into a white rumpled jersey and pair of ripped trousers. The jersey hung loosely from his torso, the black trousers digging into his waist. Then he slid on the shoes, wiping dirt and dust from them.

Moving to the bed, he sat. His eyes grew heavy, a bout of fatigue setting in. For an extended period he lay asleep, his arms flung either side, his legs wide apart. Senseless dreams flashed through his mind; images of his wife... Sebastian... space... Earth.

He awoke groggily to the roar of thunder; hours had passed. From the window he saw a glider swish by. He sat on the edge of the bed, his hands clasped together; his face gaunt, dimly alight. Walking over to a sink, he wet his face, cleansing dirt from his eyes and forehead. Then unexpectedly, he heard the front door open. Reaching for his pistol, he tiptoed to the entrance. Peering into a mirrored vase, he saw the reflection of a man walking in. Rick remained silent, his heart beating fiercely. Moving out, he took aim. With startled surprise, the man raised his hands, his face turning pale white. His bottle of white wine crashed to the ground, breaking into a shapeless mass.

"Don't shoot - please, I'm unarmed..."

The frightened man's speech was slurred, a sharp stench of alcohol seeping from his breath. Rick lowered the pistol, his shoulders sagging with relief. The aged man appeared non-threatening, his warm grey eyes reflecting a gentle nature. Across his shoulder he carried a brown satchel filled with clinking wine bottles; his face was deeply scarred, concealed in growing bristles of stubble.

"Who are you? You certainly don't look like a soldier..."

"No – No, I'm not. I'm sorry to have barged into your property."

"This isn't my property... I'm just a poor homeless drunkard. I've been here for the last few months. I've no choice; hanging around on the streets is certain death - soldiers have killed most of my friends."

Rick paused, leaning back against the wall, his mind vacant and perplexed.

"You seem to be puzzled by this, dear Sir... You're not from around here, are you?"

Suddenly there was a stir of motion and whispers from beyond the front door. At once Rick headed to the back room, the man following close behind.

"Quick, over here," the drunkard said with unusual clarity and assurance.

From the floorboards the man pulled open two flaps; a spiral stairway led to an exit at the bottom. With a crash, two soldiers burst into the apartment, their laser guns aiming menacingly. Gripping the man, Rick made his way down the stairway, shutting the flaps behind. Hurrying to the exit, with a stern shove he pushed open a small metallic door. A swirl of dust rose towards them as it loosened. Without a word the man dashed away, his legs staggering behind him unsteadily. Rick was left alone. Outside there were cries and sounds of feverish human activity echoing from the far distance. Gazing around, he sneakily darted away, moving with purpose.

At the end of the street was a group of men dressed in fine linen suits, gesturing and conversing amongst themselves. Rick remained composed, his eyes fixed on the road, trying to discard any unwanted attention. As he entered the city, the sun vanished from the sky, concealed by growing cloud formations moving above the biosphere. Gentle droplets of rain drifted down, cooling the busy metropolis. Projecting out from large advertisement boards holographic images appeared, displaying an array of newly designed air-bikes and gliders, fading away periodically. A strong whiff of cigar smoke drifted by him, fading into the air. His eyes tiredly absorbed the scene; such a drastic alteration in mankind's evolution. Rick felt alienated, unable to identify with the world he now faced. Planet Earth was no longer home. People streamed around him, hurrying past; a whole stir of commotion. He calmed himself, moving with the flow of the crowds.

Then Rick noticed a group of soldiers heading in his direction. He looked on with interest, bound by cold, twisting fear. Moving to the edge of the road he cleansed nervous sweat from his eyes and lips, congested traffic buzzing past him. Keeping inside the safety lane, he stepped back a pace and collided with a hurrying citizen.

"Hey," the man blasted, *"watch where you're going!"* Anxiously, Rick picked up pace crossing the street. People began to look towards him, pointing and curious; a few grinned in vacant amusement. His dirty tattered clothes and obvious agitation were beginning to create unwanted attention.

Peering over, he saw the soldiers crossing the street. Pushing forward in a group, one of them was holding a transmitter towards his lips. Speedily Rick dashed away, racing through a surging mass of people, panting and red-faced. The soldiers were now out of sight, lost in the growing chaos of the bustling metropolis. His dry, moisture-stripped mouth ached with thirst; avid hunger began to gnaw inside him. Down a quiet side road, Rick suddenly noticed a parked glider. Odd-looking, its sides were swollen almost to a full sphere, doors flipped open and vacant. With caution he walked over. Reaching the bonnet he paused. He turned left and right... Strangely, no one appeared to be around. Hurriedly he entered, lowering himself into the pressure seat, the belt automatically latching around his waist. Fiddling with the control dials, he then snapped on the power. The glider's engines roared into life, dials and meters swinging into activity. Moving away, he drove through the city, scattered grey clouds sweeping above. From the control console he triggered off the hover mechanism, running his fingers over the smooth metal. Within seconds it ascended, moving high above the ground, a string of vibrant lights following in its trail, glowing from the exhaust.

A lash of lightning lit the sky; a grumbling roar followed. Raising the lever, the glider steadily began to gain altitude, veering to the right. Above the radar the radio altimeter clicked, measuring the vertical distance from the ground; in green luminous digits the altitude was displayed. From the radar he detected a distant glider, the coordinates suggesting a good ten kilometres away. Across the satellite screen there was visual static. The city was now well out of sight. Ahead lay the Pacific coast; the sea was visible. Rapidly the sky broke into darkness; the clouds cleared, the moon appearing, its pale light shining above the ocean. Then a red light flashed from the control panel; an alarm sounded. A sharp metallic voice recording followed: '*Low power… Low power… Prepare emergency landing.*'

Gripping the wheel, he began a swift descent, the glider jolting fiercely as it lost power and speed. As he approached the ground, the land-lights activated, the ocean highway looming ahead. With a loud bang, it landed, showering sparks into the sky. A screeching sound followed…

Bracing himself, the glider slowly came to a halt, its engines dying into silence. A matter of seconds passed. As he pushed the door open he stepped out, sand and dust blowing around him. The sea was still, the sky pitch-black, a few stars flickering through dense clouds of ash rising from the glider's bonnet. In the gloom Rick noticed some men advancing, walking across the beach. Reaching for his pistol he held it tightly, his hands trembling nervously. As they passed through the glare of the headlights, he saw three mutants; none he recognised from his initial encounter. His heart leapt, flooding his body with fear and hope. There was a long pause, as they exchanged piercing eye contact.

"*Who are you? It's unusual to see a glider out here…*"

"*I'm in trouble… My friend has been taken away by soldiers. I need to find him…*" Rick replied, his voice stuttering with panic.

A mutant began walking over. Standing directly before him he touched Rick's face, glaring at him with curiosity and a profound perception. It was as if he could see his thoughts; as if they were written across his face.

"*What's your name?*"

"*Rick Harrington.*"

"*You're not from here… are you, Rick?*"

"No."

A gush of wind swept by; a few seconds with it.

"I'm Zane. Why don't you come back with us? We've got a settlement near here."
Rick was apprehensive, yet the mutants offered him a possibility of friendship and hope. Walking away, he was taken into an old jeep. Metal fatigue was clear and evident; corrosion too, yet it moved powerfully heading to a secluded camp, towards a bleak line of hills and beyond.

The journey passed briskly. The camp was nestled in an isolated zone concealed by a range of towering trees. The trees were hard and barren, leaves hanging lifelessly; the sound of crickets all around. Resting in a corner was a lantern shining feebly; it diffused a minimal illumination, practically nothing. Along the ground a few lizard-like reptiles crept, concealing themselves between gaping cracks and clumps of loose earth. Calmly Rick stepped out from the jeep, closing the door. His cheeks flushed a deep red.

He saw a bonfire burning brightly; twigs and leaves singeing, crackling in the heat aided with gasoline. A few mutants stood around cooking and warming themselves; the evening sky brought with it a chill. Spread around the camp lay several huts constructed from timber and thick branches; the stench of poverty and desperation in the air. An old bearded mutant limped over crookedly holding onto a crutch, its sharp point lost in the soft ground.

"Who's this?" he snapped angrily, his voice husky and almost inaudible.
"Don't worry - he's a friend," Zane replied.

Walking over, Rick gazed around. A faint breeze blew against him, his fears now subsiding. Reaching the bonfire, he knelt down, his eyes slanting with fatigue. Slowly Zane approached him, a few curious mutants following behind. They watched eagerly, faces alive with hope and fear.

"Bring some food for our friend!"
At once a young female mutant came over holding a plate of rice and meat. Hunger-stricken, Rick ate, pouring it down with cold water. A deep shadow was cast under his hollowed-out cheeks, as a fiery light shone across his face.

"Rick...if your friend is still alive, he's probably been taken to the Terra Base prison in Sacramento."
Silently he absorbed the words, running his dirt-stained hand through his hair.

"Yes, that's right - the military had sentenced us to be detained there; luckily, I got away. Tell me, am I the first human you have befriended?"
"You talk as if we weren't human! It seems that you're unaware of certain facts. Rick, we may have evolved differently, but we are Homo sapiens just like you. After

the initial blast, some of the survivors were left deserted on the streets in poverty. Most suffered the effects of radiation. Subsequently, all the children born showed neural characteristics of a radically different kind; somewhat startling. After hundreds of years, a human mutant came into being. Now, in answer to your question: Yes, you are the only non-mutant that we have embraced within our community. Rick, why is it that you talk as if you were from another world? You seem lost and startled."

"Now's not the time, but I will explain... Trust me, I will."

Zane smiled.

"Perhaps in the morning we can speak more. For now I'm going to leave you; I'm in need of rest. We'll talk at sunrise."

Standing up, Zane walked away, the other mutants following behind. Unbeknownst to Rick, he was revered amongst them. A man of his stature offered valuable gnosis; higher intellectual knowledge; an insight to the outside world - at least, that's what they hoped. He broke their tradition; they needed to integrate a new way of life into their own... After all, these people lived like primitives within a world of such advanced technological know-how. Such a sharp contrast; almost inconceivable...

He was now completely alone, staring out into the distance, the night sky engulfing him. The only sound came from the licking crackles of fire; somewhat calming. Lying in the corner he spotted a dog asleep, flies crawling around its lean flanks.

Suddenly the sky clouded over; the cold orb of the moon vanished, a flock of immense birds crossing the horizon, flying silently. Torrential rain began to fall. Rising to his feet he walked into a hut, a secure shelter from the rain. Inside it was dull, the only light source coming from two large candles covered in lumps of melted wax. Old pieces of furniture lay around; beds, chairs and tables. A group of mutants were sleeping soundlessly.

Before long he lay asleep on a bed, hunched up in a heap. Outside it was silent but for the relentless rainstorm; rain mixed with particles, lethal dust still falling. In the morning Rick awoke, the hut empty, sounds of laughter ringing in his ears and the chattering murmur of voices drifting back and forth. Rubbing his eyes, he walked out squinting from the sun's rays, adjusting himself to the light. A glowing trail of red smoke slit across the sky, fading away into the morning air. A group of young mutants sat playing in a pool of mud, an old mutant gazing over them. Resting on a stone table was a block of hydro slag, used to fashion weapons.

The steaming earth was wet with moisture from the downpour. The soggy ground crawled with insects and bugs, colourful distinctive kinds of which he had never seen. Lifeless leaves moved and rustled as underground creatures burrowed sullenly away from the burning sunlight. There were endless varieties of life.

Up ahead, Zane came rushing over.

"I hope you slept well; the rainstorm was pretty bad. Rick, we need to talk. A friend of mine wants to meet you; he's waiting in that hut over there..."

Stepping into the hut, Rick saw a mutant working under the light of an arc lamp. All around lay electronic equipment, a maze of wires and circuitry. In his hands he held parts of a disassembled firing mechanism, studying it intently.

He was dressed in an old tattered soldier's uniform; a large woven belt supported his sagging ripped trousers, a loaded pistol slot to the side. There was one specific characteristic that differentiated him; he was abnormally tall for a mutant. The mutant looked up, full of stubborn dignity. Slowly he began to walk over. Meeting an outsider promoted the wrong kind of emotions in him; he was not accustomed to it.

"Rick, this is Lando..."

"I've heard a lot about you."

He reached out his hand; they shook - a warm greeting.

"Tell me, why was your friend taken by the military? Was he a rebel, or is there some other hidden motive?"

Brushing his hand across his face, Rick was forced to unveil the inevitable; a colossal task. Pulling a chair, he sat.

"It's a tall order to explain the unexplainable. I'm not going to mix my words: I'm from another time; another world. Earth was once home to me..."

The mutants stood open-mouthed, expressionless with startled apprehension.

"I left Earth in the year 2400 on a space mission around the solar system with my co-pilot. On our return we had to make an emergency landing. Before long, we realised that we were in another time... another world. Over six hundred years have elapsed. Somehow we were catapulted ahead in time. I don't know how or what, but what I'm telling you is the truth, as unbelievable as it may sound. I'm now on the run, accused of being an alien - an alien spy. To cut the story short, I've also lost my friend; he has been taken away by the military..."

Lando was silent; a strange expression had come over his face.

"It's quite an astonishing sequence of events. Despite that, something tells me that you are being honest - what other objective would you have for such a bizarre story?

There is something oddly different about you, Rick... I couldn't pinpoint it. Tell me, what was the world like in your time?"

"Peaceful. There was harmony amongst fellow men. Our challenges and dreams gravitated around conquering space. Yes, there were world tensions, rumours of wars - political strain, as there has been from when time began - but nothing like this. The war has left marks of destruction everywhere. A reflection of man's innate destructive tendencies, it's now a planet ridden with ruin, radiation and death..."

There was a pause.

"Zane tells me that your friend is detained at the Terra Base prison. We can help you find him."

"Why do you want to help me?"

"Months ago I was imprisoned there. Took me two years to break out. Unfortunately, many other innocent mutants remain captive, deprived of their lives, never to see the light of day, amongst others and all those who oppose the system - a communist system; an iron hand which is determined to inflict pain and control over us. Rick, I have no other motive - only one based on sentiment. Tomorrow at dawn we'll head there. It's located in Sacramento - a fair drive."

From his pocket he pulled out an intricate-looking device.

"Take this, it might come of use."

"What is it?" Rick asked bluntly.

"It's a special device which we have used to gather important information against the military and against the government. We do have some sophisticated equipment in here..."

Rick was confused, his eyes cold and hard as he returned the mutant's level gaze.

"I'm not sure I know what you mean."

"It's a communication tool; a channel bug. It's able to pick up wave frequencies, which allows us to tap into conversations some hundreds of miles away - a valuable tool. For the most part, the channel bug works..."

Rick began to examine it, turning and twisting it in profound curiosity.

"I see that you come heavily prepared."

"Yes, we do," Lando replied flatly.

"Tell me... How do you suggest we break into the prison?"

"You have only one real possibility. The prison is heavily surveyed with special cameras and laser detectors. To get past that is merely impossible. Then you've got advanced robot guards which have been programmed to shoot and kill on sight; mechanical exterminators. The only chance you have - a slim chance, at best - is for you to go in as one of the guards..."

For a moment there was silence. Rick stood in deep concentration. In his mind he knew that it was a gamble, yet one he was prepared to take. He had nothing else to strive for but to find his friend.

"It's the only way, Rick. It's up to you. I can supply you with a uniform, as well as a special electronic card which will see you into the prison safely. We've had all the equipment here for some time. The card will act as your pass; it will enable you to deactivate all the locks, giving you access to the cells and exit points."

"But how will I be able to locate my friend?"

"Inside the prison there are special data systems. The card will activate them, supplying you with the necessary information."

"And what about getting out of the prison?"

Rick's voice rose, ceasing abruptly. Pensively he stood, gazing at Lando.

"That's up to you. It won't be easy... Do you want our help or not?"

"I guess the circumstances are overriding my emotions. I have no option but to find my friend."

"Okay; we leave tomorrow. For now, I suggest you spend the day relaxing. We've a long, hard journey ahead. Nearby, there's a stream. Go there, it will help you reflect - ease your mind."

As the day slipped by, Rick stood silently by a small narrow stream, his tortured mind flooding with memories; memories that brought burning tears of sadness and desperation. There was nothing to console him, yet the desire to see his friend again burned inside him like an unquenchable fire. Out in the distance he noticed a section of the ground had been broken up. It appeared as if a machine was embedded in the ground; some kind of advanced excavation tool. A line of cavities stretched on; miles of dead lifeless trees...a barren wasteland.

At the crack of dawn Rick was up, heading out of the hut. He had spent much of the night in deep thought. The early morning twilight was ignited with residuals of lingering smoke, left from wandering spacecraft. Beyond the hills the sun was rising slowly, shedding a mild heat, fowls in the air gliding above. Ahead Zane came strolling over, full of humility; his face had a peculiar glow about it.

"Morning, Rick. Are you ready?"

"Yes. How many of us are going?"

"Only three... Me, you and Lando."

Lando came walking over holding a map, his black boots trudging against the earth, twigs and branches breaking under his weight.

"Rick, this is a detailed map of the prison; take a close look so that you're familiar with its layout."

Grabbing the map, Rick paused. An intense expression of concentration set across his face; his eyes roamed as he took in the information.

"I'm ready - let's get going," he said, his voice faint and dry like rustling weeds.

Stepping into the jeep, they were on their way, heading down the Pacific coast. Particles of sand blew through the air insistently, moving and whipping against the arid landscape, a vast wilderness without limit or end. In the sky was a bird; a large eagle-like creature hovering and dipping through the air, its great wings beating with frantic haste. Rick gazed in fascination at its large wingspan; it was distinctive and colourful. They drove on heading East, away from the coast, passing through miles of untamed land. The scorching sun's rays were glowing down; it was bare and lifeless. In the distance stood a towering range of red sandstone hills; ragged, untouched and rich in iron-oxide. Shielding himself from the sun, he began changing into a uniform; not quite the perfect fit, as it dug tightly around his body. He then slipped into a pair of shiny black boots. Silently he began studying the map, stretching the corners flat against the seat, indenting the areas of importance with his nail.

Over six hours had passed; a long, tiresome journey. A little way ahead stood the city of Sacramento, a city which was heavily bombarded with ongoing earthquakes and tremors. The surface of the land was pocked with great gaping sores; huge cracks formed from the constant movement of tectonic plates. Before the war it had been an industrial city bubbling with activity, filled with towering buildings. Very little of that was now left. Far off, in the distance, a white glare burned. Luminous smoke rose from it. Veering to the side of the road, Lando stopped the jeep, the wheels grinding. Turning, he focused his attention towards Rick.

"We're only twenty minutes away now. The prison is situated on the outskirts of the city. All of the guards come into the prison from glider buses; it's for security reasons. Further on there's a check-in-point; that's where we will leave you."

Rick was silent, digesting the information, calculating a strategy. His mind was in overload, his eyes stern and pensive.

"Here, take this. It's a small chip; a tracking device. It will enable us to locate you. Once you're out of the prison we will be waiting..."

Taking the chip, he examined it with meticulous precision. It was a simple pin-shaped metal thread, flexible with a miniature receptor emitting a red pulse of light. In the air there was a feeling of dread and tension, almost tangible. Swallowing hard, Rick wiped his forehead with a piece of loose cloth. Grabbing the steering wheel, Lando headed down the road a few miles further, looking around vigilantly. Steadily they entered the outskirts of the city, an area littered with homeless people and crumbling ruins.

A mist of particles was rising through the atmosphere; a rancid smell hung in the air. In the distance Lando saw a group of prison guards standing and conversing. Swiftly he pulled the jeep to the side, halting abruptly beside a dead tree stump.

"Right…this is as far as we can go. We could get stopped and questioned; it's far too dangerous. From here you can make your way down to the far end of the road. Look, you can vaguely see the check-in point from here."

A strange cold sensation came over Rick as he sat absorbing the information. He felt faint. Everything around him went into a blur. Shaking his head, it cleared slowly. He began to regain poise, condensing his thoughts into a semblance of rationality. Lando turned to him.

"Good luck, Rick…" He smiled - a broken smile.

Opening the door, he stepped out onto the hot gravel. He began fastening the small needle-like chip into his shirt. As the window opened Zane held out his hand; Rick moved over, gripping it tightly. He was silent, the numbing emotion leaving him at a loss for words, yet in his glowing eyes the muted urgency could be seen rolling through his mind, straining and breaking him - the growing fear was agonising. Briskly he moved away, walking towards the group of guards at the far end of the road. Behind him Lando drove, heading in the opposite direction. Deep down Rick was wrestling with conflicting emotions, yet his path and mind were set.

Minutes had passed. A little further stood the check-in point, a large metallic-structured shelter. Gazing around, he noticed some old ruins; metal frames from demolished buildings jutted up from the ground, black ash and dust moving towards the sky. In the corner a tyreless wheel lay in a heap of rusting machinery, sparkling faintly in the sunlight. Across a ragged rock a lizard scuttled, disappearing into the ground.

His eyes scanned the landscape inquisitively. Rick increased his pace, kicking piles of debris out of his way, his heartbeat pulsating from the side of his neck. On the ground, covered in gravel and ants, lay a decaying robot; its brain cage was smashed open, a maze of wires and circuits gaping out. He was curious. Walking over to the inert machine, he knelt down prodding its rusting mechanical brain with his finger. It swung aside; an electrical impulse. More wiring became visible, intricate and complex - somewhat baffling. Inside, through its crushed breastplate he noticed infinite relays and switches, fine wires almost invisible to the eye. Rising to his feet, he dusted himself down and moved on.

Before he knew it, he had reached the group of guards. Suddenly they turned, staring towards him, pausing briefly in their discussions. With apprehension he moved forward, his hands quivering uncontrollably. They stood rigid, alert; no reaction other than the odd faint whisper. They were more concerned with their late-night exploits as they began chattering away, breaking into fits of laughter. He took a deep breath; the heat was increasing, somewhat hotter than usual. Then, from the distance a green glider bus approached, hovering steadily above the ground. Within seconds it had reached the spot, coming to a halt, its engines whining into silence. The metal doors slid open, retracting back. Stationed at the front was an armed soldier, a pair of slender line binoculars around his neck, a robot driver seated close by.

Rick remained immobile as the group of prison guards scuffled to the front of the bus. Slowly, one by one, each guard entered, sliding their identification cards through a detector machine. Finally, he was the last to enter; his heart beat ever increasing, his lips twitching nervously. Holding the card with a trembling hand, he slid it through the slot. The machine bleeped; a green light followed. Turning away, a metal bar dropped in front of him - a robot safety control. The soldier prodded him on the arm. He turned.

"May I see your card, please?"

Rick stuttered, stepping back. Instantly he tried to regain his cool, placing the card into the soldier's hand. The soldier gazed at him for a time looking repeatedly at his pass, rocking back on his heels.

"Your face isn't familiar... You must have been newly recruited, I guess?"
"Indeed..."

The soldier smirked, returning the card. As the control bar lifted, Rick slowly made his way to the back of the bus, sitting on a row of empty seats. Within a short time he saw the Terra Base prison ahead, a huge structure reinforced with towering metal bars.

It was constructed from special alloys which enabled it to absorb shock waves from the ongoing earth tremors; it was an area of high geological activity. Outside was a group of patrolling robots, their steel frames sparkling brilliantly in the midday sun. The robots were programmed to eliminate any trespassers; they were without emotion, a task best suited to them.

The bus began to lose speed, its powerful hover mechanism dying slowly until it came to a halt. Two identical-looking robots approached, moving in a mechanical motion, their metal faces cold and inexpressive. As the doors slid open, they walked in holding laser guns of a slender shape. Stretching out its right arm, one of the robots pulled out a retractable wire transmitter from its twisted metallic frame. He raised it towards its mouth, holding it in his manual grippers of a fingeroid shape. To Rick's surprise it began to speak with a human-like voice, refined and clear. It was a peculiar sight; these inanimate machines were able to communicate, make decisions, think and act accordingly.

Rick sat agitated and fearful, yet cohesive in his thoughts, the palms of his hands hot with sweat. With a sudden command the robots ordered the guards to leave the bus and commence their daily duties. Cautiously he rose from his seat, moving forward. Passing the two robots, they turned, eyes dilated wide with perceptive awareness.

Walking to the prison entrance he followed behind the group of guards. He loosened his collar; the effects of the heat were now taking their toll. He was weak; his throat dry and coarse, stripped of its moisture. Entering, he stood back absorbing the scene; a futuristic prison teeming with robots, machines and other mechanical devices. The floor was made from white stone, a chalky white. Large cameras lay sealed against the ceiling, revolving in continuous motion. Fluorescent lights lit the prison; towering pillars lay fixed in each corner shining a grey metal. His eyes wandered curiously, his mind engaged on the task at hand.

At the back of a long hallway he noticed a silver control unit. Nervously he reached for his card, clutching it tightly in his hand. He waited, standing still as a group of guards strutted by. Calming himself, he moved forward, striding down the hall; sharp and attentive, bright overhead light shining across him. As he reached the spot he stopped. Holding the card, he swiped it through the control unit. Instantly a green light flashed. He blinked; the small computer screen shone, humming into activity. A penetrating mechanical voice sounded.

"Welcome 4-40E... ENTER IDENTIFICATION NUMBER..."

A string of computerised sounds followed. Rapidly he punched in his identification number and then spun a dial; within seconds he was entering the database.

Across the screen was a 3-D model of the prison; a rolling device enabled him to magnify it accordingly. Anxiously he began accessing the necessary information. It was a telling moment - a moment of truth. After all, it was down to chance; Rick wasn't certain that Sebastian was alive or indeed in the prison. After a few nerve-racking moments he located him. He was partially relieved - the next bit would be more challenging.

The screen read: SEBASTIAN CASSIDY-CELL 40-THIRD FLOOR. Pressing the clear button, the screen began to fade. A red light flashed as it deactivated.

With a shaky hand he rubbed his eyes and then headed towards the end of the hall, his footsteps echoing with each stride. Finally, he reached the elevators. Pausing, he took a breath; a long, steady breath. With speed he evaluated the situation. He became increasingly concerned; the entire complex was filled with patrolling guards and cameras. It seemed to be an almost impossible mission to accomplish.

As the elevator doors opened, he entered. Standing in the corner were two soldiers dressed in dark blue uniforms, white and blue bands across their shoulders. Steadily, Rick moved over to the panel, pressing his finger against a button. The doors shut. Within seconds they were heading to the third floor. Surprisingly, the soldiers remained quiet. They didn't mutter a word; they seemed uninterested in where the elevator was going. After what felt like an eternity, the elevator stopped. Before he could move, the soldiers rushed ahead of him. He paused, waiting patiently.

A drop of nervous sweat dripped from his forehead, trickling down his cheek. Stepping out, he glanced either side. To the right, at the bottom of the hall was a large barred door; it was the entrance to the cells. Cold air blew towards him, moving out from the walls; hidden ventilators regulated the temperature and cleansed the air. Before he could move, a guard approached him from behind. His face was slashed with scars, the whites of his eyes faded in with his pale blue pupils.

"Are you looking for someone? Have you been ordered to patrol this zone?"

Faintly, Rick replied, "Yes... I was given orders."

"Can I see your identification card?"

Silently, he held the card towards the guard. Mental strain was now building, bursting loose inside him; it was becoming increasingly difficult to camouflage his obvious fear and anxiety. The guard remained still, staring at him. Rick's breathing grew irregular, his heart pounding in and out of rhythm. Lowering his collar, he wiped away perspiration from his neck.

"Okay 4-40E, I'm sure you know your duties. Get going…"
The guard then turned and walked away, heading into the control room. Rick was overcome with relief, but the mission was far from over. Reaching the entrance to the cells, he deactivated the lock. The barred door clicked open. He edged his way forward, looking around with caution. The path was clear; no one in sight. Focusing ahead, Rick noticed several cameras emitting a small beam of light. He stopped. He heard a sound; a whirring sound. Turning, he saw a voice recorder connected to the wall; it was used to regulate and monitor the guards as well as the prisoners. Moving a little further, the shiny steel floor suddenly diffused a white light, an unearthly radiation seemingly without source; a highly developed X-ray device. He paused, his eyes bulging with startled surprise.

Composing himself, he rubbed his forehead reflectively; an easy escape didn't seem probable. He walked on, glancing at each chamber. All were sealed off with thick titanium doors of a rusted colour. Above was a liquid crystal screen, numbering each cell in numerical sequence. Steadily he moved along, feeling his way forward until he finally reached cell 40. Passing his card over a code beam, the code signal registered, releasing the lock. Inch by inch the door opened until it came to a halt. Switching his eyes nervously, he silently slipped into the cell, forcing the door into a semi-closed position. A strong smell of stagnant water drifted to him. In the corner he noticed a pipe protruding from the wall; droplets of water dripping relentlessly onto the floor. Lying on a bed was Sebastian, silent and still, a ripped, stained sheet cover lying across his lame, beaten body. He moved over.

"Sebastian, it's me…"
His dark sunken eyes opened; he was overcome with emotion, chapped lips twitching in disbelief, his mouth sour and dry. His face was yellow, faintly luminous, ravaged with fatigue and fever; his body sweat filled with odour.

With a frail, husky voice, he spoke out.
"Rick - I can't believe it… How did you get here?"
"Hurry, I've no time for explanations."
The beating sound of heavy footsteps and muffled voices drowned out his words. The guards were now alerted to his presence and intentions; the presence of an intruder.
"Damn, we need to get out quick…"
Before Rick could move, Sebastian held him feebly by the arm.

"Rick, listen to me. There's nowhere to go. Don't you remember what you told me? That blinding light - how we were catapulted ahead in time? Can't you see; logic and natural laws dictate that we shouldn't be here - in this world, in this period of time we don't exist... Ever since they took me away, I've had this feeling that I don't belong..."

Rick's eyes widened with assuming knowledge.

"Whatever happened to us as we entered the earth's atmosphere shifted us ahead in time; some kind of chronological disorder - a time warp. Up there in the vastness of space there are mysteries far beyond human comprehension... Time has now caught up with us."

There was motion outside the cell; a group of soldiers arriving, laser guns loaded and pointing. Swiftly Rick drew his pistol and clutched it tightly, aiming it towards the door, his hand trembling with trepidation. Suddenly the cell door opened. Squeezing the trigger, he stopped - there was no one. Cold fear swept over him as he lowered his pistol. Turning, he reached towards Sebastian, but the bed was empty, the sheet covers warm and creased. There was total silence; a cold silence, just the sound of confusion resonating in his mind. Gazing around the empty cell, he walked out, a dazed expression of confusion and uncertainty set across his face; his mouth gaped. The prison was lifeless, void and empty; yet the same metal structure was still in place. Nothing had altered. Rushing to the elevators, he turned from left to right. His face, suffused now with growing horror, continued to twist and work spasmodically.

"Sebastian...! Sebastian...!"

His voice boomed and echoed up and down the hallway. There was no reply but for the sound of his own echoes. Reaching ground level, he fled through the exit; clouds of dust rolled across the ground, blown by the wind. At that moment he stopped, as if his feet had sunken into the ground with immediate effect. He became motionless, stiffening into a paralysed immobility. The wind blew around him. Above he saw the burning sun. His dry lips began to twitch, the heat from his body dissipating. Falling to his knees, he raised his hands. Slowly, he began to fade, fading into the dimness beyond...

"Sir, this is Colonel McGowan. We've searched everywhere... Scanned the desert for miles; still no trace of Rick and Sebastian, apart from a space helmet and an oxygen tank..."

The line broke off abruptly; he gripped the transmitter. There was a static sound then a faint muffled voice, cold and neural, followed by silence...

Behind, a rescue worker came racing over.

"Colonel, a strange-looking craft was spotted just a few miles away."

A great sun-darkening object flew overhead. They turned...

The Storm Chaser

THE sky was illuminating white light with the cracking sound of thunder. It was late night; the drenched highway was dim and obscure. The headlights flickered feebly in the darkness; there was an ominous silence, a faint mist rising through the air.

Steadily, I journeyed from Boston to Pittsburgh *en route* to film a tornado. As a child I had always had a sub-rational craving for adventure. The journey through Pennsylvania had been a spectacle of endless narrow valleys, breath-taking hills and fertile fields; the distinct contrast in topography was a captivating sight. From the surrounding forests a cold gush of air swept onto the highway, glancing vacantly into the distant horizon. I could barely make out the road ahead, due to the intense rain. A sudden ring distracted me. Raising my cell phone, I answered.

"Hey, Al… How far are you?"

His voice was somewhat muffled and faint.

"Mike, I can just about hear you… I'm around three hours away; this damn rainstorm is really delaying me. Are you with the rest of the crew?"

"Yeah, they're here. Oh, by the way, have you heard from Rachel yet?"

"No, still nothing; it's been a couple of days now."

"Strange…"

"Mike, the signal is really bad; the line keeps breaking. I'll call you when I get closer to Pittsburgh."

The phone went dead; there was no signal.

In the distance cars were now coming to a halt; an obstruction signal flashed ahead. Pressing my foot against the brakes, the van began slowing down, stopping behind a row of cars. Then, from seemingly nowhere, a sturdy-looking police officer walked over to me holding a flashlight, pointing it in my direction. His clothes were saturated in rainwater. Leaning into the window, he smiled.

"Sir, I'm afraid the highway has been closed due to the storm. It's just a precaution. You'll have to turn back or take one of the side roads."

"Great, that's just what I needed…"

Without reply, the officer walked away, trying to appease a number of grumbling drivers. Heading off, I was hoping to see a nearby exit as I had no intention of driving back to where I had come from. A whip of lightning flashed across the skyline, radiating light onto the outstretched highway.

From the corner of my eye I vaguely distinguished a small slip road. Contemplating my options, I decided to take it, uncertain of where it would lead. Hurriedly, I made my way.

The long narrow road was bare and dark; not a car in sight. Even the rustling of animals was lacking; nothing stirred. I was tense and agitated. Leaning back, I searched for a sign post; there was nothing. In the dense gloom of night a sudden flicker of light alerted me. Gradually I came to a halt, guided by my curiosity. As I looked over, a car was parked to the side of the road. Proceeding from the darkness was the figure of a tall young woman. Lowering the window, freezing air streamed in, bringing with it an array of country aromas. Hurriedly she approached, her footsteps trudging in the rain-drenched road. Her eyes gleamed with fear, a fear that seemed to exude from her being. In the glare of the headlights, her face contorted with delirious panic. With a sharp piercing voice she spoke out.

"Mister, you've got to help me! I've been stranded here for hours; hardly any cars have passed. I'm out of gas, and I've just heard the latest weather warning on the radio..."

She paused, panting heavily. Her long eyelashes flickered with dismay, rainwater dripping from her nose.

"That freak tornado - it's on its way; they estimated it will hit within the hour. We have very little time - it's now heading for Harrisburg."

"Miss, calm down. Get in, I'll give you a ride."

She moved blindly, lost in a haze of confusion and terror. Entering the van, she sank into the chair; folding her arms, she shielded herself from the numbing cold. Her lean fragile body quivered; she coughed, swallowing hard.

"Sir, we need to move - we are running out of time. We've got to find somewhere safe!"

Briskly I headed away, gaining speed, somewhat baffled by the shocking news. As a storm chaser, it was my job to regulate the movements of tornadoes. I swiftly came to the realisation that this one was subject to sporadic changes, different to the others I had encountered. Not only had the tornado rerouted, but it was now due to hit within the next hour - it exceeded all expectations.

Increasing the velocity, the van swayed and bounced, splashing through a multitude of puddles and wet dirt. A burst of frigid wind moved across the road, gathering fallen leaves with it. In the depths of my mind there was a feeling of urgency. I was compelled; I needed to get the girl to a safe place, yet I had to remain focused. Time was of the essence. Harrisburg had to be no more than a few miles away. Reaching for the cell phone to call Mike, it rang before I could dial.

"Al, can you hear me?"

"Just about."

"Have you heard the news? The tornado is now heading for Harrisburg. I don't know what's going on; I don't think I'll be able to get there. It's under an hour away from hitting the town centre."

"I know, Mike. Look, I'll have to go alone; I can't let this one slip by me."

"Are you insane? Forget it man, it's far too dangerous. We already knew that this tornado was out of the ordinary; it's exceeding speeds of 600 kilometres an hour. You can't possibly work alone; besides, it will be dark when it strikes."

For a moment I paused. Mike was right, it was a highly dangerous situation - yet one in which I was prepared to gamble.

"Listen to me - we've both seen some incredible storms, but none of this magnitude. It's a once in a lifetime; it's the ultimate storm. I can't let it slip away... I've got all the necessary equipment here; trust me, I can do it alone. Besides, all the stations will pay megabucks for a few seconds of footage."

"Al, listen... Listen to me! It's been travelling from the southern part of the states since this morning gaining, speed and momentum; it's already destroyed countless towns and cities."

Mike's voice was high-pitched and strained; his obvious distress rippled from inside him.

"I know what I am doing, Mike - I'm no novice."

"Whatever you say, just be careful... I'll call you later."

The roaring thunder echoed in the darkness, leaving a frightful aura in the atmosphere.

A signpost loomed further on; it read: 'Harrisburg 1 mile.' My main objective was to get the lady to a strong shelter; at least, somewhere safe. Uncertain of where to take her, I contemplated various possibilities. An evacuation didn't seem probable; Harrisburg was the only option. Sitting there, the lady was motionless; her hands firmly gripped the seat, her smooth skin red from the cold. Placing my arm across her shoulders, I tried to comfort her with a smile.

"Miss, sit tight. It's going to be okay, I promise you. I'll make sure you'll get somewhere safe."

Soundlessly, with a subtle gesture, the lady appeared to acknowledge what I had told her. Entering the city, we were welcomed with an eerie silence; the only sound coming from the battering rain and the howling wind. The streets were desolate and bare.

Suddenly, a jeep pulled out, swerving to the side of the van. Nestled inside was a group people. From the jeep a man stepped out; his raincoat was soaked, his face pale and fearful.

"Hey mister, you need to find some shelter immediately. A tornado is heading this way! Come with us; there's a huge sports centre. Most of the people in this town have taken refuge there."

As I lowered the window, I could feel the tension in the air. Hurriedly, I replied.

"Sir, I'll be okay; however, you can take this young lady with you."

Turning to me, she smiled, her face pale and drawn.

"I don't know how to thank you - or what to say. Please, be careful…"

Closing the door, she raced towards the jeep, her hair rumpling in the wind. As the jeep's engine sounded, the man turned to me, accelerating into the distance.

From the sky I heard the piercing sound of helicopter propellers, its lights fading and flickering in the darkness, twisting in a circular motion. It seemed to be patrolling the city; probably to make certain that everyone was seeking shelter. I paused. The task at hand was going to require finite timing. Working alone wasn't exactly the easiest thing to do, especially in such irregular circumstances. Heading to a country road, I pulled to the side of an open field. Along the edge of the field was a grove of old withered trees, some bent and leaning, torn loose from the stony soil by the endless howling wind. Calmly I mounted the video recorder, assembling all the appropriate machinery and checking the temperature gauge. Outside the ice-cold weather was now beginning to take effect. My fingertips grew numb; my feet cold and rigid - a lack of circulation.

Gripped with apprehension, I sat fixed to the seat, waiting, my heart fluttering with nervous excitement. Time elapsed and there was no sign of the tornado, hours drifting by. Reaching for the phone I tried dialling Mike's number, but there was no signal. The satellite systems were down; even the Doppler-radar was unable to pick up any kind of frequency. Nervously I switched on the radio in an attempt to pinpoint the problem. There was nothing, only static… I stood back perplexed; something was wrong.

It was now 4.50 am. The rain began to ease, and the darkness was slowly fading, breaking into light. For a minute there was silence. Suddenly in the distance the tornado approached; a monstrous supercell swirling through the atmosphere. The huge vortex reverberated sounds like a raging sea, ready to devour anything that stood in its path, the vibrations shaking the ground beneath; it was simply inexpressible. Luminous columns of white light flashed ahead as it tore through power cables. Cars were lifted high off the ground, swirling above in the air; hailstones streamed down pelting heavily against the vast landscape, crashing into a shapeless mass.

Above the supercell was an electric thunderstorm. Each whip of lightning lit the sky an intense white, yet there was something almost unearthly about it. I was left captivated, my eyes staring in awe and reverence. Positioning the video recorder I focused in, capturing images of the sight, a mixed feeling of fear and euphoria emanating from within me. Then at once, the tornado seemed to shift, changing direction. Turning the key in the ignition the van jolted into life, a strong smell of fumes rushing towards me. Squeezing the accelerator I gained speed. My mind was set; I was determined to keep within its range.

A powerful wind surged against the van. Turning, I saw the tornado moving in my direction. In an instant I lost control, swerving into a tree at high velocity. On impact thick grey clouds of smoke filled the surrounding air. I couldn't see, the dense smoke totally blurring my sight.

Panic-stricken, I attempted to start the van, twisting the key in the ignition, but it was no use; the engine had been badly damaged. Turning, I saw it; only a few hundred metres away and gaining power and momentum as it majestically tore through the fields. A vicious burst of wind struck the van, spraying shards of broken glass and pieces of debris at me. Overwhelmed with fear, I lay pinned to the seat staring at this awesome act of nature that was ready to devour me. Closing my eyes, I thought this was to be my last breath. Suddenly, the tornado hit…

I awoke lying in a hospital bed. Only moments ago I had stood face to face with a tornado; I couldn't conceive how I had survived. Startled, I was left searching for answers. Gazing around, I felt an emptiness, the like of which I had never experienced. A feeling of urgency reverberated within me. I needed to speak with someone; someone who could offer an explanation for the bizarre events that had unfolded. With a great effort I pulled myself out of bed, latching to the wall for support. My head felt heavy; my bones ached with intensity. Inching my way to the door, I soon realised it had been tightly locked. It was firm, unmovable. Nervous agitation fumed within me; I simply couldn't conceive why.

As I turned, making my way to the bed, I saw a pile of pamphlets and papers scattered across a small plastic cabinet; a broken brown cord lay above. The walls were covered with anatomy charts; somewhat odd for a private room. Peering through the window, I noticed a tall concrete building; a towering column of steel and cement. A team of construction workers toiling unremittingly in the cold dusty air. Loose metal pipes and planks of lumber lay sprawled across the site, dirt swaying in the wind.

Shaking my head warily, I encircled the room. I tried to reason as to how I had got here - such a sudden twist of events. It was pointless; I just couldn't recall what had happened. It was a gap I was desperately searching to fill. A spasm of pain rippled inside me. I felt faint, cold sweat breaking out across my forehead... Suddenly, from the corner of my eye, I was captivated by an image; an image so clear and real. Across the front cover of one the papers was the photo of a man bearing an incredible resemblance to me. I rubbed my eyes, looking over again - it was there; not a figment of my imagination, as I had hoped for.

Hesitantly I walked over, my eyes wide with fascination. Lifting the paper, I held it close, and there - there it was; a photo of me, just as I had seen. It was unmistakable. Pausing for breath, I was left stifled. This was not possible; it had to be a fabrication of the mind. In bold letters the article read: *'Fugitive Al Dennis captured during a police chase.'*

Tearing the article from the paper, I placed it in my pocket. At that moment my thoughts were interrupted by sounds of echoing footsteps, each step growing louder, each step in rhythm with my pulsating heartbeat. The door opened; a tall thin doctor walked in accompanied by two police officers. Turning, I froze, standing dead on the spot.

"I'm Doctor Clinton. I see you're feeling better, Mr Dennis. You've made quite a considerable recovery in such a short period. Soon enough you will be discharged."

His deep-sunken eyes sparkled and the trace of a smile twitched across his lips. Moving to the bed, he began checking the readings on the various machines and instruments.

"It looks like you're doing better than I expected. Your body temperature and blood pressure have stabilised significantly; all we are waiting for now are the results of your tests. Anyway, I'd better leave you with the two officers; I believe they have some questions for you."

Walking to the door, the doctor left. It went quiet. As I gazed vacantly towards the two officers, one of the men approached me, holding onto his belt.

"Mr Dennis, as soon as you are discharged you will be taken down to the FBI offices."

"What are you talking about? Why...?

Cold autumn air rushed in through the open window as the two officers stood there staring at me with penetrating eyes, their faces devoid of sympathy.

"Mr Dennis, I think it would be easier on yourself if you quit messing around and playing games; it's in your best interest to comply with us. I suggest that you start to come to terms with the inevitable..."

I was overwhelmed with uncontrollable emotion as the reality of it all came hurtling down on me. I began beating my fists against the wall in an attempt to relieve the psychological turmoil that was now building within my mind.

"Mr Dennis, I'd advise you to calm down, otherwise you will force us to take you away immediately. Mr Dennis, I will not repeat myself."

Overtaken with panic, I reached for a large wooden chair, swinging it ferociously towards the officers; the breaking impact caused one of the men to fall to the ground, sprawling to his hands and knees. Impulsively the other officer raised his pistol, taking aim. His face was twisted with rage, his eyes lightless; there was nothing there, only fury beaming from him. Pulling out a set of handcuffs, he forced me against the cold concrete wall. Instantly, I swung my elbow towards his head, dropping him to the ground motionless. As the gun clattered against the floor a bullet fired towards the window. With a crash it shattered into pieces, showering the room with glass. Within seconds an alarm activated; the sounds of murmurs and footsteps followed. Assessing the various possible ways of an escape, it seemed the only way out would be to exit through the shattered window. Stepping over shards of broken glass, I rapidly made my way over. The wind suddenly surged against me, whipping the freezing air towards my face. Nearing closer to the edge, I glimpsed down below, noticing a tree standing to the side of the building. A scraping sound from behind distracted me. Turning, I saw the officers moving across the ground, reaching for their pistols. In a flash the door swung wide open. Bracing myself, I jumped...

A burst of adrenaline raced through me as I landed awkwardly on the tree, gripping to a large forked branch. A mass of cobwebs and dusty leaves covered my face, blurring my sight momentarily. Pulling myself into a stable position, I gasped for breath, my lungs labouring painfully. Across the street the group of builders stood staring and pointing.

Beneath lay a long wide road, nothing in sight for miles. Suddenly a red truck advanced out of nowhere, belching filth into the air. This was a chance to get away. Holding my breath, I waited for the moment - finally it came. As I leapt from the tree I crashed into a bundle of hay at the back of the truck. The rest was a blur...

The sound of squeaking wheels and engine fumes awoke me. Rubbing my hand across my eyes I cleared my vision, powerful engine vibrations juddering through me. Up ahead the moonlight slanted down towards a country road, casting a glowing reflection of light. I was engulfed by infinite green fields broken by the occasional farm building; darkness was rapidly descending. A few stars glittered distantly, scattered clouds wandering to and fro. Pulling myself from the hay I paused in my thoughts, mystified by the sequence of events. Steadily the truck began to lose speed, retreating into a small avenue covered in old lifeless trees. In the gloom the trees appeared stern and menacing; the air was dense and misty. Through the haze stood an old cottage, a lamp lighting the porch. A wooden stairway led to the door. Lying in the grass was on old decaying fence, broken and splintered. As the truck door squeaked open, the driver leapt out, strolling leisurely towards the cottage and rattling his key chain. As he reached the door, he unlocked it, disappearing inside. From the darkness, a car advanced, slowly coming to a halt beside the truck. Two men stepped out, probably detectives, dressed in long dark overcoats. For a time they stood watchfully, exchanging words. Then, abruptly, they began heading towards the cottage. Before they could reach it, the truck driver walked out. Minutes passed, yet it felt like hours. After a discussion, the two men moved away, switching on flashlights and walking directly towards the truck. Before they could reach it, I managed to slip away, hiding behind a tree.

Kneeling on the ground, there was a foul smell of rotten vegetation; underfoot a cascade of debris spilled around my feet. Overhead an aircraft was flying by, the sound of its engines roaring dimly. The two detectives leapt onto the truck and began to investigate. Suddenly, there was a rustling sound. A small fox rushed past me; instantly they both turned, focusing the light in my direction. Concealed by the darkness I lay still, my heart hammering wildly as small droplets of sweat dripped from my brow. After what seemed an eternity they walked away, heading towards the porch where the driver stood. It went very quiet. I could hear the odd faint murmur being exchanged; what, exactly, I couldn't tell.

Within minutes, the two men drove off, leaving the smell of car fumes in their trail. The cold wind gushed through the towering trees filling the air with a musky stench. As I peered towards the porch, the truck driver was heading to the door. At that moment, it began to rain, hammering down hard. Gripping the tree, I moved forward, one step at a time, my eyes wandering nervously, shifting in all directions.

Inch by inch I moved almost calculatingly, but then I lost my footing, falling heavily to the ground. It went silent; dead silent. I looked over as the man raced over. He opened his mouth to speak but no words came out. He stood there cold and rigid. At that moment I had no alternative but to confront him. His old tattered clothes and menacing appearance indicated to me that he wasn't exactly the kind of man who could be bargained with.

"Sir, listen to me please…"

The man remained hushed; not a word came from him, but with his eyes he signalled his intent. Rushing to the truck he pulled out a rifle, his face flushed with exasperation. Hurriedly he slid a fresh round of bullets into place and then slowly began to approach me, taking aim. His face was vacant of emotion. Standing still, a paralysing fear passed through me. Instantly I leapt towards him.

In a frantic struggle, I managed to pull the rifle from his grip, throwing it towards the deserted road. Then I swung my fist, connecting with his jaw. He fell to the ground, lying there in a helpless heap. Gasping for breath, the reality of my predicament flashed before me. I closed my eyes, overcome with exhaustion. I was sapped dry and lifeless, but I had to keep going. Around me I was confronted with a dark, desolate landscape; one which would lead nowhere. Suddenly the sky lit up, a ripple of lightning cracking loudly followed by complete darkness - space without depth. Gazing up towards the elements, the formless unstable clouds seemed to separate, and re-emerge. I stood watching this peculiar sight, as the rainwater fell relentlessly against me. Clutching the set of keys from the dirt, I headed into the truck, wiping damp grass from my hands. I was soaked, my jeans drenched with rainwater. The truck windscreen was badly cracked; pieces of glass lay sprawled across the dashboard. Even the odometer appeared to be out of function.

Holding the steering wheel, I slid the key into the ignition. It jammed. After several attempts the engine juddered into life, spraying exhaust fumes into the damp night sky. Hurriedly I was on my way, speeding down the road.

As the night slipped by, the rain began to ease. A short way ahead stood the town centre, lights flickering, shining faintly. From far away I heard the sound of a passing train, a gloomy wail echoing through the darkness. Outside the air was crisp, filled with the fragrance of floral perfume, gathered in by winds from distant fields. Peering into the mirror my face was drenched with sweat, my shirt torn and blood stained.

Miles of untamed road had passed me; no signs of life, not even the occasional car. With care I drove forwards; the road twisted and began to rise. A little further on it levelled out. I could now see a group people vaguely ahead. Steadily the truck began losing speed. A red light flashed signalling low fuel; the motor began groaning. Finally it stopped dead, the engine shuddering to a halt. Outside, a few metres away, stood a small gas station; to the side a phone booth, people walking by. Racing towards the phone I found some loose change scattered across the floor. Who could I call? Dialling Mike's number, the phone rang, my hands trembling as I eagerly awaited a response. It gave me a flicker of hope.

"*Mike, it's me… It's me - Al!!*"

"*Who? I think you've got the wrong number…*"

"*Wait, please, don't hang up. It's Al - Al Dennis; don't you recognise my voice?*"

There was no response; the phone slammed shut. I remained still, my mind an empty space, unable to conceive what was happening. Frustration soon grew into uncontrollable rage; a rage which I could no longer constrain. Not even my closest friend knew me… *Where was I? How did I get here? What now?* Barging through the glass doors I noticed a gas station attendant pointing. He appeared startled; dropping his tool box, he fled towards the shop. Then by the gas pumps I saw the same lady I had picked up on the night of the storm. Everything about her was the same; her clothes, her hair - it was as if I was reliving that very moment. With urgency, I raced over towards her. As she turned I grabbed her by the arm, that same fearful face staring back at me.

"*Miss - It's me, don't you remember?*"

She was cold and unresponsive.

"*You must remember! Your car was out of gas; I picked you up on the night of the storm.*"

Leaning back, she pulled her arm loose from my grip.

"*Mister, I have never seen you before!*"

Gazing into her eyes, my mind was taken back to the night of the storm. In a matter of seconds a police van drove into the gas station swerving violently, the screeching sound piercing and sharp. Close behind two police cars followed, a cop half-dangling from the window. Besieged with fear I had no option but to force the lady into the car, driving away speedily. The lady sat there, her hands clenched tightly on either shoulder, her face drained of its colour, tears burning in her eyes.

"What do you want from me? Please don't hurt me - I'll do whatever you want!"

Her croaky voice was drowned out by a loud shattering roar. Behind the police were gaining speed, coming closer, battering through cars and signposts. Nervous fear was swelling in me, churning inside. In a moment of compassion I swerved the car, stopping instantly.

"Quick, get out! Come on - hurry!"

Soundlessly the lady left, slamming the door behind her, disappearing into the night's darkness. Securing the safety belt I gripped the steering wheel and accelerated, driving away in a quick burst of speed. As I looked into the rear view mirror, police cars were closing in on me, their headlights shining brighter as they moved closer.

Bullets began pelting into the car, rupturing parts of the engine. A strong smell of gasoline filled the air, sharp and toxic. In rapid succession I lane-hopped until I got ahead, avoiding further gunfire. Then another police car directly on my right swerved, losing speed and control, crashing into a field. Gripping the steering wheel I could feel the cold metal under my fingers. Sharply I cut into the left lane between two cars; the road was now clear.

Looming in the far distance was a barrier of police cars; lights beaming wickedly, officers scattered across the ground. Within seconds they opened fire; instinctively I squeezed the accelerator. Before long I was within close proximity of the police…inching closer and closer. With a loud violent crash I hit the barrier of cars, the momentum catapulting me into the air; the car landing awkwardly on the other side of the road, wheels and bolts spraying in all directions. A towering column of smoke rose from the engine, evaporating into the atmosphere; flames blazed up rising rapidly, showering sparks into the air. Pulling myself from the raging flames of fire, I lay on the ground, my vision dim, the faint sound of sirens echoing, dying softly into the evening sky.

Next I awoke, music ringing in my ears, the van radio playing. A strong smell of engine fuel filled my nose. I was disoriented, unaware of my surroundings; a bout of dizziness hung over me. Raising my head from the dashboard, my face was caressed by a gentle breeze as warm air swept in through the broken window. Ahead, a police car raced over; with it, I felt the colour from my face drain. Fear threatened to overwhelm me.

Veering to the left, the car slid to a halt, its siren whirring into silence. The door opened. Missing his footing, a cop stumbled out; in a frantic haste he came over to me. He had a bland ample face, the appearance of a young teen.

"Sir? Sir, are you ok? You are so lucky to be alive. I'll get you some help. The paramedics may have to come by air."

Running towards the car, he clutched his phone. Then suddenly I realised I was back. Turning around, I was filled with elation. I was back - back on the same country road where the tornado had struck. I just couldn't believe it. Conversely, I was left puzzled. It was unconceivable; there was just no feasible explanation. Was it a dream, a hallucination? It seemed so real; I could recall every little intricate detail, details that one couldn't usually recall from a dream. Perhaps something bizarre had occurred in the tornado, something which connected with the orderly flow of time. It was pointless wracking my brain; it was all just hypothetical logic. I needed something more concrete. A sudden ring broke my thought pattern. Pulling the phone towards me, I answered.

"Al? It's me: Mike. I can't believe you've answered! I was so worried. I have tried calling so many times; are you ok? I really feared the worst. What happened? Did you manage to film the tornado?"

Hearing that Mike recognised me was a great relief; however, I didn't know how to respond. I felt somewhat constrained to reveal the truth to him, as he could never begin to fully comprehend what had really transpired.

"Mike, now's not the time. Believe me, it's a long story. Look, I'll call you back in a bit... Give me a couple of hours."

As I sat gazing into the distance, I heard the sound of propellers descending from above; the sound intensified as a helicopter landed. Coming out of the van I made my way through endless piles of debris. Rocks and lumps of loose earth lay splattered across the road. The morning air was heavy with the smell of burning rubble, tinged with a whiff of country odours. Rushing over to me came a team of paramedics clutching onto a stretcher.

"Are you okay, Sir? You shouldn't be moving. It's an absolute miracle you survived; this is one of the worst-hit areas. I just can't believe you're in one piece. You literally went through the eye of the storm."

Before I could reply, the paramedics guided me into the helicopter. Within minutes we were airborne, flying high above the ground. Sunlight brightly lit the horizon and beyond as I sat trying to distract myself from the deafening sound of the propellers. Staring down below, the land had been left desolate and barren, flattened by the powerful tornado which had caused a wave of destruction. Debris were scattered throughout the land for miles; trees torn from the earth, thick black smoke ascending into the air from wrecked buildings and torn power cables, ash, dust and chaos. Captivated by the scene, I was left breathless, lost in my thoughts and gazing at the desolate expanse. Within no time, I lay seated inside a busy hospital ward, mayhem and confusion surrounding me, sounds and noises clattering in the background. To the front stood a row of chairs filled with patients; a ghastly sight.

Resting my hand against my forehead, I began to ponder... Could my mind have conjured up such a dream? The complex mysteries of the mind could project all kinds of images; images that could seem real. Perhaps the tornado had opened up a doorway to another dimension, a parallel dimension; an alternate reality....quantum mechanics. Slowly my thoughts began to fade, winking out of my mind. After seeing the doctor I headed out of the building, passing through a crowd of visitors and convalescent patients. A restless stir moved through the hallway. Forcing my weight against the door, I emerged into the main lobby moving towards the terrace. Outside the air was chill, a whiff of cool air brushing by me. In the distance I noticed a team of firefighters working away tirelessly, removing pieces of debris. Across the street were the remains of a ruined motorcycle, a charred wreck. I could sense the desolation of the landscape in the air, it became almost tangible. At that moment my phone rang.

"Hey Al... I've just arrived back, how are you? I've missed you so much! I tried calling you countless times but the lines were down. Are you okay?"

Taking a long steady breath I replied.

"I think so... Well... When I see you I'll explain. Listen, Rachael, I'm in Harrisburg Pennsylvania; I'm going to get a flight out to Boston tonight. Hopefully there won't be any delays..."

"That's fine... Can't wait to see you! Call me as soon as you land."

As I closed the phone, a warm sensation swept through me, her voice soothing my troubled mind. Leaning back, my eyes began to drift, gazing into the pale blue sky. At that moment I decided that the sequence of events which had transpired would be kept secret within me forever.

A couple of days had flashed by after returning to Boston. All the vivid images of the storm which had been deeply embedded in my mind were now fading. I felt re-energised. Conversely, a part of me was still in a desperate search for answers. As I lay resting, puffing away at my cigarette, Rachel was preparing tea. Reaching over to the side cabinet, I stubbed out my cigarette into the glass ashtray. The bedroom was warm and peaceful. Through the half-closed drapes I saw the sun hanging low in the sky, a cheering start to the day. Staggering out of bed, I slipped into a robe, switching off the gas heater in the corner. As I walked towards the kitchen, I could hear the radio blasting out music; through the patio window sounds of early morning activity. Swinging the door open, I entered. Standing there was Rachael, a look of bewilderment and curiosity beaming from her dark eyes. Silently I stood, staring towards her with expectancy.

"Al, I just found this bizarre newspaper article in your pocket: Fugitive Al Dennis…"

No Mars Redemption

Gary Pope sat at the kitchen table in fear. The inevitable awaited. His eyes roamed, gazing intensely at the rusty red landscape in search of refuge. "Hun, wake up...!" his wife Zena chimed. "Still fighting it?" His cold eyes deflected away from the oblong-shaped window. Thick glass divided the poisonous world that was Mars from the enclosed oxygen world.

"I just can't accept it... One month to go...." he paused in subdued acceptance; his lips twitched. "One month before retirement... If only I could get my hands on those government officials, I'd-"

"Hun, there's no way out. Forty is the retirement age for us Androids. Besides, to get a maximum life extension of ten years will cost too much. Remember; we were built together as a pair, built for one another. I'm not extending, so even if you could - what would be the point?"

He stormed out and headed to the mood regulator in the hallway. There he dialled exactly what he wanted. A needle plugged out from the machine, piercing into his palm. Briskly it pumped in the narcotic calmer. He drew breath, and exhaled as the drug took effect. The mood regulator buzzed, indicating completion of its task. The needle retracted for concealment.

He was now on a train, heading to the Mars city centre, bright Martian light reflecting across his pale face. Next year was going to be the big year. Mars would have its own natural source of air. The enclosed world would be no more. But he wouldn't be there to see it. Out in the distance, jets hovered above the Martian world. Yellowish flickers of light blinked on and off. Across from him an advertisement video-screen flashed into life. Words appeared: 'Memories are important. It's the past that shapes our present...'

Suddenly a figure approached. "Gary...."

"Tony! You still around?"

"Yes, I managed to pay for an extension... Sadly, Rebecca declined. You?"

"No. One month more, and then..."

"Hey, come on... Us andys have to accept it - ten years in addition or not - we all meet the same fate. Even the humans have an expiry date; maybe not by law, but inevitably they will all die at some point."

"It's just not fair, Tony. We should have the same rights as them. Why us - why me? Perhaps locating the inbuilt termination device and manipulating it somehow could extend my life..."

"Possible, but pointless. Apparently, some andys claim that there's a matrix fitted within us; a grid screen that cuts us off from certain actions and thoughts - a programming mechanism which controls us. Some claim that if we found the programming circuit we could manipulate it in such a way that we could then be in control of our reality - a subjective one - thus gaining complete homeostatic functioning. Even if true, being aware makes all the difference... Perhaps this termination device is somehow interlinked?"

"Maybe, Tony... But whether in complete control or not, all I want is more life - yet I have no control over it."

"Does anyone?" Tony asked rhetorically, wide-eyed. He then pulled out a digital-card, peering quickly behind his broad shoulder. A number lay across it, luminous and inviting.

"Here - take this. He can help you. He helped me, but whatever you do, say nothing to anyone."

"Who can help me? How...?"

"Just call the number - trust me."

Gary gazed out, his thoughts drifting into the dusty, tawny carbon-dioxide nitrogen atmosphere.

It was now night. Darkness had descended over the face of the planet. Gary sat alone in a bar, thinking about his discussion with Tony, the overhead light emitting a variation of colours that shone across his face in a quasi-orderly pattern. In the background an elderly couple muttered away, dialoguing about the new oxygenised Mars that was to come and how all the Martian fauna and protozoa would probably die, unable to adjust to the new atmosphere. Gary absorbed bits of it here and there, toying with the digital-card, his face curious. *I need to call and see what this is all about,* he thought. *Perhaps the termination device is located somewhere within my mechanical brain... But even then, who could help me manipulate it? It would require a technician...Yes, a technician...This has to be a number to some kind of technician.* He stopped his introspection and stood. Slowly, he made his way over to the corner of the bar, and there he halted beside a digi-phone. Across from him, in the amber gloom, an advertisement flashed from the 3-D Tel-set, which hung seemingly in isolated suspension. 'Objective reality is built upon the foundation of a multitude of subjective realities which in turn form a universal concept.' The words faded and a music video began.

He held the card anxiously, sliding it into the digi-phone. The line buzzed and clicked as the circuit was established.

"Hello, Mr Pope," the touch digi-card relayed the info of the caller, via skin contact, to the receiver.

"Hi. I'm calling about..." he looked over his shoulder, "I was given your number by..."

"Mr Pope, say no more. Meet me now at the Olympus Apartments, room 8."

The call cut sharply. Across the digi-phone, the word CRYONICS appeared in big letters; a number followed. Gary looked away with distaste; after all, cryonics was reserved for humans only. Regaining his composure, he stood for a time thinking and biting at his lip. The bar and the gaudy opaque shapes of people faded before him into a blur. Then, within seconds, he was on his way to meet the unknown man, still uncertain of what he could offer.

He now stood outside the apartment door. Pressing the buzzer, he immediately heard footsteps. The door opened via a mechanical arm.

"Quickly, come in, Mr Pope," the casually dressed man uttered sharply, his cold blue eyes piercing.

Gary walked into the apartment promptly, gazing around the room. There was a musty stench. *Probably a faulty air pump*, he thought. Across a glass table a thick academic text-book rested, titled *Fluctuations in Interstellar Magnetic Fields*. In the far corner of the room was a steel robot. It caught his intention. It was lifeless, inoperative; obviously the cleaning maid.

"Right, Mr Pope, let's locate the termination device... That is why you are here...right?

Gary smiled. At once he realised what Tony had meant. This is what he wanted. His eyes said it all with muted clarity.

"I'm Carl Jones - an ex-doctor. Spent many years in research down on Earth. You obviously know this is an illegal operation. By all means, pass on my information, but be very careful who you tell - this is top secret."

"Yes, of course, don't worry."

"I've worked on at least twenty others, all at a fixed rate of 500 Mars Dollars. That betters the 5000 that the government charges by some margin. I take it your partner's not interested...?"

Gary's face dropped. Carl immediately perceived.

"Seems always to be the same. All those with partners never convinced the female to extend; they always opted out. All the andys I've worked on have been male... But one thing I'll tell you is that many have felt a void when their partner ceased... However, an extension of ten years of life is worth everything - right?"

A moment of silence passed.

"Yes... Yes, it is. I've longed for years to see the new Mars - this is the only way to make it possible."

"Good. Let's proceed..."

Gary now stood under a specialised x-ray device located in a lab within the apartment. With the turning of a switch a screen flashed into life, and there before him was his biomechanical anatomy, intricate and baffling.

"That's me...?"

"Yes, Mr Pope, that's you. Don't worry, most andys are taken aback initially. Ok, I have located the termination device. Every Android is built differently. Do you see that green squared pulsing light in your brain?"

Gary looked at the screen nervously. The mood indicator bleeped. A small screen activated, relaying his emotions in the form of waves; high frequency waves.

"Yes."

"That's it - located right next to the programming mechanism which controls your thoughts and actions."

Gary began thinking about the discussion he'd had with Tony. "So - I'm not in control?" he muttered to himself almost inaudibly. "What's that above it?"

"T-roll."

"T-roll... What's that?"

"Tape-roll - the reality supply construct device that is fed into a tiny scanner, then into your central nervous system. All your sense stimuli come from that unit."

"Wait a second... If I was to remove that unit, my world would end? My reality?"

"Yes, Mr Pope. It controls all the encephalic processes. You seem perturbed; you're not the first - many andys become confused when they see what they are really made of..."

Gary stared at the screen, eyes wide and intense. He could see flesh-organs all interlinked with highly developed machinery; wiring, bolts and screws finely assembled. His heart sank. He looked on, mesmerised by his pulmonary system; a network of flesh and metal. *What am I?* he thought. *What really controls all of this? Am I real? What induces sleep? My dreams... What are they - are they programmes too?*

Seconds of silence passed.

"Right, Mr Pope. When would you like to proceed?"

Gary walked out of the silver metallic x-ray device. He rubbed his jaw in thought.

"Sorry, just need some time to gather my thoughts... It's been quite an experience."

"For sure, Mr Pope, but I wouldn't look too deeply into it. This is the usual reaction I get...but it will pass. Your world is important to you, right? It's all relative. That's all that matters, surely?"

Gary stood in a hypnotic-like silence absorbing the words uttered.

"I'll be in touch... Need a few days."

He was now at home, in his kitchen, gazing out towards the lifeless dark landscape, sipping a cold double shot of Russian vodka. His wife Zena lay asleep in bed. His meeting with Carl was eating away at him. Deep thoughts continued to surge through his mind. *I knew I wasn't human...but...but an inanimate object? Why exist? Better that I'd never existed... Why an extension of life? 'Life' being the operative word... I'm not real...or am I, partially? Do I really exist? What's the point of it all? Is anything real around me - my feelings towards my wife; life - everything? Even my desire to see the new Mars can't be real. My world, my universe is controlled... I'm not in control at all. To gain true homeostatic functioning would require being human, period - nothing else. An extension of life? For what? It's pointless.* The sudden psychological transition was too much for him to bear. He looked at the digi-card for the last time. Standing, he headed to bed, walking into the semi-darkness of the room...

Time Report

The Time Report was completed, filed. Reinhardt Brewster sat contemplating the two-hour dialogue he'd had with the authorities, his old eyes calm and satisfied.

A sudden knock at the door startled him. *It isn't the regular thing to get a visit at this hour*, he thought. Opening the door, he saw a young man standing before him dressed in a light grey suit.

"Mr Brewster?"

"Yes."

"We need to talk."

"Who are you?"

"Please, it's important..."

Without reply, Reinhardt signalled the man in.

"Take a seat."

The man walked in, then made his way over to the sofa and sat.

"Mr Brewster, I believe you've completed the Time Report?"

"Doesn't everyone, once they reach 65 years of age? It's the only way to obtain an approval to live out the rest of your life - die naturally. I've been approved. My good life, my good deeds have merited it."

"Good deeds... According to whom, Sir?"

Reinhardt sat with interest.

"What do you mean?"

"Mr Brewster, I've come here with a very important message. As you know, we live in an atheistic and pantheistic society. Although both appear to have opposing views, they are really one and the same, and both are very wrong. Both philosophies have been indoctrinated to the world with severe consequences."

"Please continue..." Reinhardt muttered, shocked but overwhelmed with intrigue.

"To remove God from our lives is man's greatest mistake. Pantheism teaches us that nature, the universe and the totality of everything is God. In other words, God is part of creation, and that everything - including mankind - is part of God. That makes no sense; by definition, God means the eternal being that created, and is clearly distinct from, creation. If God is part of creation, he's not God... Thus, it makes no sense to suggest such a thing. In fact, pantheism and atheism are the same, only pantheism tries to disguise its atheistic philosophy by misusing the word 'God' to mask its true outlook on life. Atheism teaches us that God doesn't exist and that we just evolved... In other words, out of nothing came everything - a mindless explosion brought everything into existence; set life into motion. Logic tells us that this is impossible. The same logical deduction may be applied to various occurrences. If a hurricane swept through a junkyard, would you expect to find a perfectly working spaceship left behind? The answer is clearly no. Yet atheists teach this by asserting that an explosion out of nothingness shaped and formed our Universe and life as we know it. The existence of the Universe can only be explained by accepting theism; monotheism. How else can the existence of the universe be explained? Remember, all events have causes. The highly questionable theory, known as the big bang theory, claims that all matter in the Universe was condensed into a point initially. The question is "Who created that point if that was indeed the way life came into being?" You see, it makes no sense. Even if the theory were true, you still need a creator. So how did the Universe and existence come into being? There are three possibilities: either it came into existence out of nothing, or in other words it was spontaneously generated. The second possibility is that it always existed, and the third is that it was created. To assume that the Universe, which is composed of mass/matter/energy, just spontaneously came into being is absolutely absurd... In fact, it violates the first law of thermodynamics, which governs the behaviour of energy. The first law of thermodynamics is a fundamental law which helps us understand and explain our Universe and is diametrically opposed to the whole notion of a spontaneously generated universe; a universe that appeared from nothing. This complex, baffling universe could not have come into existence without the presence and intervention of a supreme being; a force that lies way beyond our physical universe. Hence, the Universe must have been created by a non-physical force; a force that dwells in eternity. Only God has the power to bring life into existence out of nothingness. To assume otherwise defies all logic."

Seconds of silence followed.

"Now, regarding the notion of the eternal existence of the Universe, the eternity of matter... The first and second laws of thermodynamics show that the Universe was created. The laws suggest and tell us that there had to be a beginning - a creation. Everything around us is subject to erosion and decay (entropy); the cycle of life. Look within our cosmos: stars live and die as they lose energy; we live and die. Conclusion - the Universe and everything in it had a beginning. Just think logically: if the Universe were infinitely old; that is, eternal, it would have reached a point where all usable energy was exhausted, but science shows that we are not in this state. Hence, the Universe is not eternal. Also, if the Universe were infinitely old, it would be infinitely large, which it is not. Now that we have established that the Universe had a beginning, logic dictates that there must be a single uncaused cause of the Universe. The uncaused cause of the Universe is obviously greater than the Universe it brought into existence and is distinctly separate from it, opposing all pantheistic views. The uncaused cause cannot be part of the Universe; a universe which had a beginning and is finite. The uncaused cause has to be an infinite being, infinite in both space and time, holding the universe of matter and all existence together. This is God. God exists independent of the Universe; independent from its laws. All logic and reason tells us this. God is outside of the Universe; an omnipotent, eternal, all-loving being - one in essence, yet three in personality. The work of the triune God is seen even through the design of the Universe itself; a Universe that is made up of all Space, all Matter, and all Time - a tri-universe of Space, Matter, and Time. In fact, Space itself is also a tri-unity, comprised of three dimensions, with each dimension permeating all space. Similarly, the same can be said of Time: future, present, and past. The same truth is applied to Matter; the unseen, omnipresent Energy that manifests itself in various forms. Even Man himself is a tri-unity; body, soul and spirit - made in the very image of God."

Reinhardt was still, absorbed in the unknown man's words.

"God is the answer; the only true, logical answer. Everything else fails, as the laws of thermodynamics prove. The spontaneously generated theory and the eternity of matter are both logically and scientifically impossible."

He paused.

"Now think about the psychological impact that atheism has on a human. Just think of the implications that come with atheism: to accept that you are just a mistake will surely affect the way you view yourself and others around you in a very negative way. It will affect your view of morality; it will affect your decisions; your mind-set as a whole. Everything becomes meaningless. Without God, we lose sight of morality... Morality and God go hand in hand. Morality has to be built around our love for God. This is the true meaning of morality. Without God, ethics and morality become subjective. This is the essence of sin, that we become dictator of what is right and wrong. Without God being at the centre of our lives, the very foundation of our being, man is lost; without hope, without direction. A closer examination into the existence of ethics and morality, the anthropological argument, reveals that there must be a God - right and wrong, good and evil. The whole purpose of life is connected to morality and ethics. Atheism equates to no purpose to life and the universe. That in turn implies that there is no purpose to morality or ethics. There are many false philosophies regarding morality, like Hedonism, Utilitarianism, Nihilism and Relativism. Without any doubt, the theocentric approach to morality is the only way to explain the purpose of life. This will automatically provide the right motivation for a genuinely ethical approach to life. We are morally sensitive. Why? God implanted this within the soul of man when he made us in his image, and God is eternally good. So why is there evil? Man was made with free will, and sadly chose to walk away from God's perfect laws. God wants us to love him freely by choice, a process that entails relationship with Him and moral obligations that go with that commitment. Biblical morality is the key. It's designed to develop within man the right attitude to life and morality. The greatest commandments are to love the Lord God with all your heart, and your neighbour as yourself. All the laws of morality and ethics are encompassed within these two commandments. This is true morality."

Outside, it began to rain hard. Reinhardt couldn't quite understand who this man was, but he remained hushed.

"The conclusion to this is mankind's moral responsibility has to be based upon the fact that God is our Creator. Since morality is grounded in the unchanging nature of God, His laws are absolute - they are not cultural; not relative; not situational. Having said this, the laws could apply differently in extreme cases. A very important - in fact, fundamental - question that needs to be addressed is: is there an ultimate consequence to immorality? An atheist and pantheist would say 'no'. The implications that come with those philosophies are very serious. It means that human existence makes no sense."

The unknown man stood, his eyes wise with profundity.

"Finally, even though God wants us to live by high moral standards, He is aware that we are frail and are subject to failing. This is why He has provided salvation; his marvellous grace is unending. He has revealed Himself. He now stands at your heart and knocks..."

Invader

The ship landed with a thud! Chris Nicholson released the lever and the hatch opened. Slowly he stepped out into the cold night darkness. Beams of ship light split sections of the blackness that engulfed him, penetrating and unveiling a rugged landscape of rock and dust. It was a monumental moment. The planet had been vigorously analysed from Earth, scan-modules in outer space filling in the missing pieces. All knowledge was attained. His assignment: explore and survey.

Activating his torch, he held it tight and tense. The torch shone brightly, cutting holes into the darkness. He waved it sporadically for a time, then walked back inside the ship and dialled. Connection was instantly established.

"Lukas; everything as expected. I'll keep you updated…"

He stared at the screen with accomplishment, once again taking in the various readings: Atmospheric, Gravity, Mean Orbital Velocity, Mass, Density, Orbital Eccentricity, and Albedo. The Planet's Albedo reading was low; sunlight obviously well absorbed by the surrounding forests and oceans.

It was daylight. A grey sky hung above him as he strode across the soft ground with his robot, five miles out from the ship. Ahead in the distance he could see miles of green. A forest of towering trees. Flowers were everywhere, blue and green alike. A primitive virgin planet with great beauty. He knelt down and ran his hand through the soil, placing some into a small plastic bag. It would be used for soil composition analysis back on Earth. Then something caught his attention, metres away. Standing, he saw what looked like a human, lying as if dead, flea-like insects buzzing around him, seeking moisture. Rapidly he rushed over and to his amazement he was staring at a human being. He was naked with a heavy beard and long hair. He detected a heartbeat from the rising and falling of his chest. *Could there be others?* he thought. Not possible. No trace of life had ever been detected, aside from flora and fauna, but this threw everything in doubt.

Back on Earth, in a Government Laboratory, Chris Nicholson stood watching Dr Bert Russell attaching electrodes to the unknown man's body. A cold beam of light fell onto the man's forehead from the Neuro-scanner above. His body moved and jerked in spasms of motion. A computer clicked and buzzed, processing information. The data attained was then displayed across a large screen: *Neuro-chemical activity: Morphology*. The doctor turned, facing Chris.

"No matter what I've tried, he doesn't respond. He's very much alive but it's as if he's in some kind of coma. Yet there appears to be no damage to the cranial region; no damage anywhere, in fact."

The Doctor cut off meditatively, his mind pulsing away.

"Are there any signs of muscular atrophy?"

"No, Chris. For a man of his height and build, there appears to be no deterioration in muscle mass."

Chris raised his hand to his chin, contemplating.

"I'll check the rest of his anatomy. Take some blood samples, cardiac readings etc. Keep doing all the tests, but he will have to wait until he breaks out of this trance before we can find out more."

Chris was now in the cafeteria, sipping a cold black coffee, staggered by the realisation of what he had found and the implications that came with it. That ubiquitous sense of achievement glazed from his eyes as he looked towards the bright yellowish sunlight that filtered through the window.

"Chris?"

Instantly he snapped out from his thought-drenched gaze and turned. Walking over to him was Lukas, his eyes large and luminous.

"How's it going?"

"Ok..."

"Any news so far? Still shocked - a human being, how's this possible?"

"I have no clue. Dr Russell is still working on him. We initially wondered whether he appeared human but was actually some kind of alien being. Once scanned internally, that possibility died. He's human alright; pulmonary system, stomach, everything in place."

"Incredible... Simply incredible. By the way, Johnson just got back from his assignment on Titan, called it a heterogeneous society. Its economy is flourishing as a result of the mass sale of hydrogen mined from the atmosphere."

"Yes I've heard...used to fuel the fusion engines of spacecraft. Huge credits, hey?"

"He's conscious!" Dr Russell's assistant yelled from across the cafeteria.

They were back inside the laboratory. The unknown man sat clothed in a white gown, his eyes half-open, vaguely conscious. Chris stood with Lukas and the doctor's assistant watching. Dr Russell sat facing the unknown man, shining a bright pencil beam light into his face. The man didn't respond, aside from closing his eyes.

"Can you hear me? My name's Doctor Russell."

There was no response. Sweat began to appear across his heavily-lined forehead.

"You are here on Earth; planet Earth. What is your name?"

The man's head swayed in and out of consciousness. Then, his lips moved but the words uttered were incomprehensible. The doctor turned to Chris and the others.

"Just as I thought; he doesn't appear to understand our language."

"Do you think he might be psychologically unhinged?" Chris asked, eyes wide.

"The Neuro-tests certainly don't indicate this," the doctor replied with brisk efficiency. "Dopamine and Serotonin levels all came through as normal... In fact, all neurotransmitter readings were perfect. He appears to have a well-balanced mind, but you never know."

Suddenly, the man spoke, his words slurred and spaced apart. But it made no sense to them. His dark, battered eyes opened, then closed. He murmured a few words then fell into an abrupt state of unconsciousness. The doctor's assistant rapidly moved in, holding and dragging him into the bed. Instantly he fitted an air-mask to his mouth. Partial consciousness was restored.

"Doctor, he speaks another language!" Chris said sharply, "I recognise it as English; it was spoken back in Ancient times - one of the main languages that they used here on the planet before all languages were censored and the One language was established..."

The doctor looked at Chris with intellectual curiosity, thalamic greed.

"Let's get the language division to come and assist us right away. The information that we can obtain could be priceless, marking a new dawn for our planet..."

Across the bed, the unknown man began to twitch and move spasmodically. His hands clenched into fists of remembrance. Perspiration surfaced around his face and body. His mind began to work, piecing together his distorted memories into a collective semblance of chronological order. Pictures began to surge through his mind. He could see planet Earth, a world governed by human activity... The past wars, the dictators who had crushed the human spirit... Communism, Nazism, the technological achievements of man. He could now see himself... His family and friends, life on Earth, the oceans, mountains, lakes and rivers.

He now pictured the Earth-destroying Asteroid that wiped out all of humanity but for the few who had left the planet in time. Nothing lived. All life ceased; oceanic and land. Dead clouds of ash and blazing fire. He pictured his ship journeying through deep space with his family, his mixed feelings and emotions, joy and sorrow... The ship landing on the earth-like alien planet... A time of adaptation to the new environment, both biologically and psychologically..... Years of struggle for survival; no meat, only vegetation to eat. Then, the deaths of those close to him; his own spared by a high-tech incubator. Millions of years of survival... The incubation period ended and he awoke and found himself alone...

Night had fallen. Manhattan New York was white with a cold winter chill. Chris arrived home tired, the automatic door swinging open. He entered the apartment, removing his jacket and throwing it across the sofa. Surrounding lights regulated into a warm dimness. He stood watching the tele-set as it activated. A news bulletin flashed before his eyes - the one he'd expected. Dr Russell appeared on the screen, document in hand.

"I have an announcement to make to all the citizens of Earth: We have found the last living human being who has survived for millions of years through a high-tech incubator. Not much more is known at present, but he is the only living survivor of our ancestors who once graced our planet!"

Visions of the Future

Lawrence Colt sat inside his ship exhausted, waiting for the queue of traffic to clear as he made his way to Earth from Titan. The Space-lanes were filled with commuter ships, their lights flashing into the vast vortex of the universe. It was a four-hour journey; billions of miles eradicated by phenomenal speeds. Out in the distance, commercial rocket freighters roared, systemically making their way to Mars, Venus and Ganymede. 'More cargo deliveries,' he thought. Then, the signal lights flashed, the traffic period was over, and at last he was on his way. He activated the auto-pilot and sat back, orientating himself as he recommenced his journey, contemplating his day. Stress levels were high, indicated by the control board reading. He ignored it and decided that silence was best, rather than having that same boring stress-releasing voice chirping away, irritating the audio regions of his brain.

He was now well on his way, gripped within the vastness of deep space, well past Saturn and Jupiter...nearing Mars. He studied the view-screen. He could see the solar system and his positioning relative to it. Suddenly, a strange feeling came upon him. His stomach turned. His face flushed red. He checked the control board for a reading: Psychosomatic/Stress. Again he ignored it. Then, out of nowhere, flashes of white phosphorescent light flashed before him in the darkness of space, battering against the reinforced body of the ship. The light grew and intensified. Space itself now appeared to be consumed by this brilliant light. He closed his eyes, hands flying to his face. All controlled atmosphere was cut off. Instantly, emergency air-pumps came into operation keeping him conscious; dimly alert. He could hear the jets whining; turbines were beginning to heat. The ship jolted and shuddered violently. It gained speed - then a tense silence, followed by complete darkness.

Lawrence awoke in a daze of timeless half-sleep. Two men stood around him, their features obscured by blurred vision as he battled to register with reality. Everything appeared misty and oblique. He rubbed his eyes. Slowly the images became clearer. Full vision was restored.

"Mr Colt, can you hear me?"

"Yes," he murmured groggily.

"You are the first man to have travelled into the future - an esoteric moment."

Lawrence's eyes widened. A burst of adrenaline roused him. He lay upright on the bed, staring at the two well-dressed men.

"What do you mean?"

"I'm Philip Doyle and this is Clarke Williams. We work for a very special firm that deals with time travel, Quantum effect."

"I'm sorry, but what's this about?" He began to gaze around the room, trying to make sense of it all.

"The democratic party contacted us with a very important assignment. They wanted to find out about the future of our solar system - a special project. We needed someone intelligent and brave, calm under pressure. Your work as a private detective caught our attention, so we chose you. After a meeting, you agreed all the terms to travel one hundred years ahead in time."

"But I don't recall any of this. I'm a private eye, yes; but the rest… How's all this possible?"

"Mr Colt, we had to erase your memory for your own good. The psychological problems that you could have suffered would have been severe as a result of the sudden transition from one reality to the other. Getting back to this reality, your time would have been a hard adjustment. Remember, the eye forms an image of the outer world, transmitting it to the brain; an immediate switch would have been dangerous. However, we have acquired all the data necessary from a time-recall device that was implanted in your head. It has supplied us with all the information needed."

"What information?"

"Our planet and all the earth colonies throughout the solar system have been governed by a democratic government, as you know. However, a new party is coming into power within the next few weeks. Their laws are based around an atheistic philosophy; it's what they call a logical system that will enhance the development of man both technologically and socially. You were sent into the future to see the outcome."

"I can't believe what I'm hearing… So what did you find out from me?"

"The effects were totally disastrous; humanity did not benefit at all. It crushed the human spirit in so many ways. Crime rose to soaring levels throughout the solar system. The street violence on Titan was so bad it needed constant police surveillance. Our planet and the other colonies like Ganymede weren't as bad, but they were still very unsafe. The price of air rocketed on Mars; those who couldn't afford to pay simply died. Divorce as a whole increased. Mental disorders rose to staggering figures, the highest on our planet. There were constant rumours of wars between the colonies, threats of total destruction, blowing each other out of existence. People lived in constant fear. As a result, people lost hope; the overall desire of man to achieve and strive for economic and intellectual success declined. It inhibited the thought of mankind as a whole. A small group of people on Titan demanded freedom of religion and expression; they were all wiped out. Fear ruled, tension and destruction everywhere. These were the results."

There was a brief silence as Lawrence absorbed the words spoken. The air was tense.

"So what will you do?" he asked plaintively. "You say that this group is coming into power very soon and that it's imminent. How can you stop this happening?"

"It's not our place to decide... The current party may make a political announcement to the public throughout the solar system via the media. They may even choose to show the images that you brought back to us. This could bring the new party to a halt. It may cause their voters to reconsider, and perhaps then something can be done."

Lawrence's eyes suddenly became distant, as if recollecting a blurred memory. At first, a fuzzed blur of seeming non-reality. Then...

"Are you okay Mr Colt?"

"Yes...yes I am, but there seems to be one thing that wasn't erased from my memory..."

The two men looked at each other, eyes curious.

"I recall a bright light engulfing me just before I awoke here... I guess my quantum journey back in time. In between, I recall seeing a beautiful place; a place of peace and love, a world seemingly beyond time and space - another dimension if you like. It was so beautiful that words can't describe it. I recall seeing a river of life, its water sparkling like crystal. It was no dream; it was what I can only describe as the ultimate reality...and certainly not part of my experience in the future. Perhaps this is the ultimate vision of what lies beyond..."

Ganymede Project

JUPTIER glowed amber in the distant horizon. Cold icy stars sparkled overhead. Isaac Shovkosky stood watching his team of robots working away feverishly, communicating like ants. He was in charge of a terraforming survey on Ganymede. He had worked on many previous projects. Planetary engineering was his expertise. Ganymede was cold. The endless icy wind blew, gnawing at him every now and then. In the distance he could hear ships leaving for Earth, robot pilots heading out for deep space.

Gathering his thoughts, he made his way into the office and sat. Isaac was no ordinary human. He had been genetically engineered, able to withstand the alien atmospheres he had encountered countless times. Ganymede and its environment was no stranger to him. He was a tall man, sharp-jawed with blond hair. His eyes blue, with deep intelligence. Activating his computer, he read through scientific data pertaining to Ganymede, the green hazy light shining across his smooth intellectual face.

Diameter: 5,268km. Composition: silicate rock water / ice. Ganymede's orbit around Jupiter: Distance 1,070,400 km.

He sat back, raised his communication module, and spoke.

"Leo, please come to the office."

The module clicked a series of times in vague static. He deactivated it, and sat upright.

Within minutes a shiny metallic robot walked in with low gravity paces. Leo was a special robot, designed with an acute intelligence; far superior to the others. It had human-like qualities, a refined sense of understanding.

"Right, Leo, from what I've seen so far, it's not going to be easy to modify Ganymede's atmosphere, surface topography, and temperature to match Earth's biosphere - along with all the other essentials for human life to exist. Let's hope we find liquid water under its surface; a saltwater ocean estimated at a drilling depth of 200km. Ganymede's strong magnetosphere gives us a significant advantage."

The robot stood silently, its mechanical brain working away, registering.

"A planetary biosphere that mimics Earth..." Isaac muttered in thought, gazing at the Albedo reading, "It'll be a challenge." He licked his lips.

"Well, we achieved it on Mars, building the atmosphere. Beneath its surface was the key; heating the planet, releasing all that carbon dioxide - initiating a greenhouse effect," the robot said, harsh and mechanical. "Terraforming Mars was amazing."

"Yes...building the atmosphere there was quite something. Venus was tough, removing most of the planet's dense carbon dioxide atmosphere, and reducing its surface temperature. Europa was the best. The presence of water was very helpful. Heating the ice, supplying oxygen through electrolysis, locally manufactured. Then of course, building the radiation deflectors - that was a major challenge. Nullifying the radiation from Jupiter was tough, but we achieved it. It's incredible to think of all our successful missions so far."

The robot sat facing Isaac. Its eye lens closed and opened in contemplation, the overhead light shining against its immense metallic body.

"Sir... I've often wondered about Earth..."

Across the desk, the audio-time-signal sounded. Instantly, Isaac silenced it. He sat back.

"What, Leo?"

"I've oftener wondered who was responsible for the planetary engineering of Earth. Its atmosphere, temperature.... All our achievements required work - labour, engineering, science, physics - but Earth..?" It raised its well-sculptured metal fingers to its face. Its hand clenched into a fist of mechanical reflection.

Isaac was taken aback. A circle of bewilderment fell. No human he had encountered in all his 40 years had ever asked this question. Then - a robot! It took the whole concept of artificial intelligence to another level.

"I'm not sure I can answer that...." he responded enigmatically. "The whole notion of the origin of life currently lies outside of human understanding."

"But humans must have searched for the answers... So much energy and thought has gone into terraforming the solar system; how is it that man has ignored such a vital question?"

"A few years ago a team of physicists build a time-machine, experts in quantum mechanics. The time-machine passed all the necessary tests, but the government never allowed it to be used. It was deemed too dangerous. The project was shut down by the GSA. They wanted to journey back in time to see if they could unravel this mystery; the mystery of life, and the formation of life on earth and its baffling design."

"Why was the project declined?" Leo asked avidly.

"Any slight alteration made in the past could alter the present - it could cause a catalytic effect that would run through time, consequently changing the world as we know it today. The GSA could not take such a risk. The presence alone of man back in time could cause an alteration in chronology."

A dense atmosphere fell as both machine and human exchanged intellectual thought.

"Has anyone given a logical opinion as to how?"

"Well, Leo... Mankind as a whole attributes it to evolution. It's a highly complex, convoluted process... But there is one man on planet earth today who claims that if evolution were true, it would surely require a force to control and guide it. He describes theistic evolution as the only plausible truth, if we did indeed evolve. Atheistic evolution makes no sense."

The robot's eyes widened.

"What do you mean exactly?"

"A Creator... There has to be a Creator. This is the implication he makes."

"But it makes sense," the robot responded, "Look at me: a robot who can think, act, move, work - artificially constructed - so why should humans believe that they didn't have a designer, a creator? Planet Earth was designed perfectly without human intervention, and all types of life exist within it; human, animal, bacteria and marine. The planetary engineering that took place is simply incredible. The only conclusion is that it had to have come from a force that lies way beyond our universe, however he chose to design it."

Isaac sat in silence. The deepness of his mind was reflected in the gleam of his eyes. His lips twisted in thought.

"Okay, Leo. Go check on the survey team - report back to me in an hour."

Instantly Leo stood and made its way out, its robotic strides fading into silence. Briskly Isaac deactivated his high-tech computer. It buzzed and clicked. Moments later, he walked out of the office and stood under the bright light which beamed down on him from the top of the metallic dome. He gazed towards the distant amber light that was Jupiter. *Mankind had achieved incredible feats,* he thought. He himself was a product of incredible human accomplishment; a genetically engineered man who could withstand all the alien worlds and environments of deep space. But there was one question that lay deep in his mind. Who was responsible for the miraculous planetary engineering of Earth? Surely, whatever created it had to be the greatest mind of all.

Ripple Effect

There was darkness - the darkness of no-time. Shifting textures of destiny flashed before him. Uncertainty surged through his mind. He selected and at once was propelled in time. The blackness dissipated. He appeared in a city under the dim sheen of starlight. A swirl of buildings lay ahead, immense and metallic. Noise radiated around him; dull echoes of activity and motion. He stood orientating himself, breathing the cold air, the sharp bitter smell of darkness. Slowly he started to walk, gripped in awe. People were everywhere. Neon lights flashed red and green; cars moved along the streets in a stir of chaotic motion. He halted, digesting the scene, his eyes absorbing every detail. A different time, a different reality... *These people aren't in existence yet...* he thought, *At least, not in my time - and yet I'm here with them, gazing into the future.*

In a burst of decisive motion, he rushed to a quiet side street. He gathered his thoughts and then pressed the time-device. Instantly he dematerialised and moved through the scattered flow of time. Blackness swirled around him. He was lost in the vacuity of time. All sound and thought was cut off. His existence was held in this gloom. Suddenly there was a flash of light. Gradually he reappeared, transforming from an oscillating haze into a flesh existence. Bruce was back...

"Amazing," his college friend Dave chirped, "It worked. So what was it like to see our city two hundred years from now?"

Bruce opened his eyes wide, his head falling back as he regained poise and adjusted to his present reality.

"Dave, it was incredible. Oklahoma City had changed - even the people were different; clothes, attitude. The whole place had a different feel to it. Whatever you do, tell no-one about this - this could become a police matter."

"Don't worry... But what if your father finds the time-device missing...?"

"He won't; he's had it hidden away for years, ever since the government banned its usage within his department in the police force."

Bruce was now on his way home, moving rapidly across the wet grass fields. Cold stars appeared and vanished periodically as foggy webs of moisture drifted across the dead, dark sky. It was silent. The silence gave him time to ponder his experience as the bitter wind blew. Reaching the main road, he signalled down a driverless-auto-cab. He jumped in, fed his c-card into the credit-scanner, lay back and was now on his way, guided by the autonomic circuit.

Within no time he was home. He closed the door and moved sluggishly towards the living room, his eyes guilt-stained. He could hear his father Trent barking at his mother. *The usual thing,* he thought.

"You should not have bothered bringing those damn Martian plants back to Earth... They're all dead. I told you that they could never adapt and adjust to the earth's gravity."

"Okay, calm down. Oh, hi sweetheart..."

"Hi mom....dad."

"How was college, son?" his dad asked, scratching his bald head.

"Good thanks..."

"Keep up the hard work, and you'll be as brilliant as your grandfather was. He was one of the top doctors in the US - a specialist in psychosomatic medicine. You'll follow on from him, let me tell you."

His dad smiled with pride, walking over to the synthetic fireplace where a bright light burned.

"Your grandfather was quite a man – ironically, a fine believer in UFOs." The warm firelight lit up his face as he knelt. "He claimed to have seen many throughout his life. I've always believed that the mind sees what it expects. I'm sure that the brain can send images to the eye. With this phenomenon, I believe that you can see things that you have programmed your mind to believe..." He shrugged philosophically.

"Will you stop just for a second?" his wife Pamela snapped. "Bruce, your father and I have finally decided to get a cat - a real one though, those pseudo life forms just don't do it for me... Besides, we can afford it – right, Trent?"

"Yes, sweetheart," he replied, rolling his eyes.

"Dinner will be ready in twenty minutes." She walked off, heading into the kitchen. Bruce's mind was elsewhere. He was already planning his next journey. He sat on the sofa rubbing his jaw. On his face appeared a mysterious expression. His eyes were fixed with a glow of concealment. *I wonder what it would be like to go back in time and see my grandfather as a teenager,* he thought. *That could be my next journey, a warm-up before I start the real thing....*

"You ok, son?"

"Yes, dad - just tired..."

From the kitchen a rich aroma of food wafted into the living room. Bruce sat in silence, calculating and considering. This was going to be his first of many journeys back in time.

The following evening Bruce was in the fields, alone, standing under the dull gleam of the moon. He had made all the necessary calculations. His eyes burned with nervous sweat. He wanted to see his grandfather as a teen, back at the old family home. He held the time-device punching in the data, his feet sinking into the soft grass mud. At once, he commenced his journey, defying the laws of time. Bruce now appeared outside the old family home in the light of day. He shook his head, regaining his composure. The surroundings were beautiful. Hills sparkled in the distance. The orb of the sun shone cool and bright. He could hear sounds of life and movement. All was so pleasing and calm.

"Amazing, my first journey back in time," he muttered. He took in a deep breath of air, and exhaled. Then he focused on his target; the family home where his grandfather grew up. He stood for a moment staring at the huge grey coloured house. The front garden was well-cultivated, filled with colourful flowers.

Slowly he walked towards the house, weighing up his options, not knowing whether to ring the bell or just hope for some random chance of seeing him. Suddenly the door swung open. A teenage boy stepped out. *Could this be him?* he thought.

"Hi...Can I help you?"

Bruce froze into immobility. His mouth opened without sound.

"I'm sorry...but who are you here to see?"

Bruce composed himself, gulping.

"Are you......are you Fredrick Shannon?" he asked in awe.

"Yes...yes, I am...but how do you know my name?"

Fredrick stood awaiting a reply in his baggy tracksuit, his blue eyes soft. Bruce groped for the correct words to utter.

"Let's just say...."

He stopped abruptly.

"I'm sorry, I have to go..."

"Hey, wait!" Fredrick shouted.

Bruce turned sharply and ran, heading towards the bottom of the street. Although it had only been a brief meeting with his grandfather-to-be, he felt a great sense of juvenile accomplishment. He hid behind a car, well out of sight, puffing and red-faced. Then, holding the time-device, he moved back through time.

Bruce was now on his way home, walking the whole distance through the cold night. He was filled with excitement, gripped in awe. *I can now travel wherever I want; next the Aztecs - or I could even visit Julius Caesar, the great*

Roman Emperor. As he approached the town centre, he soon felt that something was wrong. A feeling of dread came over him. He noticed that the entire town was somewhat different; minor alterations here and there. The wind blew hard and cold. As he approached his street he rushed to his home. It was abandoned, empty and old; a house that had been void for some time. Fear besieged him; cold, twisting terror. His face now filled with horror; it began to twist and work spasmodically. What had happened? Had a simple journey back in time altered time? Had his presence caused a never-ending time shift, altering history - his history? He checked his time-device. Its reading was accurate. He briefly wondered whether he was at the right house. He gazed around for confirmation. Indeed, he was. Slowly he walked into the empty house; no sound, other than the audible beats of his heart. The floorboards creaked. Dust circled the air. An ice-cold sensation swept through him. His mind was thrown into oblivion. Confused, he went to touch his forehead, but his hand passed through. Shocked, he froze into immobility. Gradually he began to fade, fading into a haze of non-existence...

The Winds of Mars

The burning orb of the sun beamed down, shining light across the landscape of Mars. James Anderson walked pensively, struggling to take in the thin weak air of the colonised world. The days of carrying one's portable oxygen had been over for centuries. Mars was alive. Around him Martian insects crawled and buzzed as he walked on in deep contemplation.

"Good day, Mr Anderson," the shopkeeper chirped, arranging his fruit stall.

Without reply he raised his hand in acknowledgment. All that lay fixed in his mind was death; the inevitable fate that lay ahead for every man. He'd led a life of battle and war: an ex-intergalactic soldier who had been responsible for the deaths of many. Thoughts of what lay ahead tore through his mind. Death wouldn't be far; he had reached the ripe old age of seventy-four. He had seen it all. Ahead, the Mars-Earth Distance indicator flashed, currently at the furthest point: 401 Million Kilometres. Images of Planet Earth followed on a large screen; an augmented reality. Audible words followed... *Book a trip to Planet Earth and see its amazing beauty!*

Reaching the open park, he made his way over to a bench and sat gazing towards Olympus Mons. It towered high, piercing into the atmosphere. It evoked memories of the Martian wars; countless lives lost during intergalactic battles. The wind blew around him. Its sound stimulated even deeper thought. He pondered recalling the deep discussion he'd had with a Christian philosopher. He pictured the ninety-year-old man, his long white beard, penetrating eyes that conveyed wisdom... He began to relive the dialogue within the confines of his mind....his own opening words...

"What is the true meaning of life? Why death? From where did our universe originate? All the philosophers I encountered never truly answered these questions...their responses were built around conjecture, speculation and subjective opinion. I guess that mankind has always had the tendency to view life through the grid of their mind-set, but there has to be one absolute truth as to why."

"Mr Anderson, let me begin by saying that death leads to two eternal realities, two separate eternal realities. It is here where we choose our ultimate destination. This choice is made through forgiveness and coming to God. The Genesis of life is God. His word, the Bible, starts from the very beginning and takes us to the end of the universe and beyond. It is a collection of 66 books, made up of different genres; history, poetry, prophecy... It's God's revelation of Himself to man; this revelation is given through the human phenomena of the natural world. The history in the bible is history written from God's point of view. God selects what is important to Him - the things that matter to Him; events that affected Him most - and relays this information to us. But the two main themes in the Bible are: what has gone wrong with the world; and how can it be put right? Genesis explains the ultimate questions of life; why we die, and how it all began. Science has explained so much regarding the universe, the physical laws that govern the cosmos, yet it has been unable to go beyond. Science doesn't give a purpose for this universe coming into being. It can give details of how it came about but not why. Science doesn't answer the problem of evil. Science is based on steps of faith; hypothesis, theories. Science is transitional; it evolves as human knowledge expands. The approach of faith is actually scientific. The Bible fills in the missing pieces that science and philosophy can't explain. It starts with the beginning of time and finishes describing the end of the universe and goes even beyond that. The Book of Revelation gives details regarding the end of man. Eschatology, a branch of study within Christian theology, deals with this whole notion of end times - the ultimate destiny of humanity - death, the afterlife, heaven and hell. "

"Tell me about the Creator."

"Triune-theism is the God that the Bible reveals as the Creator of all. The Trinity is something that cannot be explained. It appears to be mathematically impossible; that is, 1+1+1 doesn't equate to one but three. However, if you use a multiplication sign, the outcome is very different; that is, 1x1x1=1. The universe is actually a trinity; a tri-universe of space, time and matter, each permeating and representing the whole. The universe is all space, all time and all matter - a space-matter-time continuum. Space is invisible; the background to everything, Matter reveals the reality of the universe, and Time pertains to the events occurring within the universe. The imprint of a triune God is clear to see within creation, etched into the very fabric of the universe itself. Now, from a biblical perspective: in Genesis the word used for God is Elohim, which is a plural word. "Let Us make man in Our image", and God (singular) made man in His image. There are many examples like this in the Old Testament, clearly indicating that there is indeed a trinity."

"So God is eternal?"

"Yes, Mr Anderson. The fundamental assumption of the Bible is God exists eternally. He doesn't need to be explained but what does need to be explained is the existence of everything else, contrary to modern thinking. That is, people want an explanation for God's existence. The creation suggests God must be personal, having thoughts and feelings. He must be powerful, eternal, creative, orderly... The symmetry and mathematics of the universe would suggest this."

"What about the other philosophies?"

"All the other philosophies are out of line with biblical Christianity. Atheism: no god; Agnosticism: not sure; Pantheism: all is God; Monism: matter and spirit are one; Mysticism: only spirit is real; Materialism: only matter is real; Rationalism: reason is God; Animism: spirits are gods; Polytheism: many gods; Dualism: two gods, bad and good; Deism: creator can't control; Humanism: man is god; Existentialism: experience is god. Biblical philosophy is based on Triune-theism; the trinity. One God, yet three in personality."

"So tell me, what went wrong with man?"

"In Genesis we see that there are two trees; sacramental trees, trees that had deep spiritual effects. The sacramental principle is that God uses the physical to communicate the spiritual. The tree of life tells us that Adam and Eve were not immortal, but were capable of being immortal. In other words, they would not have lived forever by some inherent quality of their own, but by having access to the tree of life they could go on living forever. No scientist has discovered why we die. Science is trying to discover the elixir of life. The secret was in the tree of life; God was making it possible for humans to live forever by putting that tree in the garden. So man wasn't inherently immortal but could become so by feeding on God's constant support of life. The other tree; the tree of knowledge, knowledge means experience. God didn't want us to know good and evil. God wanted man to retain his innocence. We have all lost our innocence. The tree of knowledge signified one fundamental point; that is, God retained absolute moral authority over man. In other words, God tells us what is right and what is wrong. He retains the right to tell us what is good and bad. But sadly, man wants to make that decision. God warns that if you break that harmony, you will die. Once mankind experienced evil, God had to limit the length of our life on earth, otherwise evil would become eternal.... Mr Anderson, it is now that you need to make that choice to know God. He will forgive all those who come to Him..."

James stood up, gazing into the atmosphere as the wind blew around him. He had recollected the whole conversation in his mind. It was time to make the ultimate decision...

QUANTUM CHRONICLES 2

Out Now   £9.95

ISBN: 978-1-84549-507-7

arima publishing